SECOND CHANCES

BOOK 2 OF THE FOREWARNED SERIES

A. K. GENTRY

BRUSHY MOUNTAIN PUBLICATIONS

ISBN printed: 979-8-9888618-8-1

ISBN digital: 979-8-9888618-9-8

Library of Congress Number: 2025924830

Book Cover by Marissa Mueller at MAM Crafted: Instragram @mamcrafted1

Editing by Margaret Griffin at margaretgriffinbooks@gmail.com

CONTENTS

Note to the Reader

Second Chances is the second book in the Forewarned Series. While it can be read as a stand alone novel, there are references to events in *Unprepared*, Book 1 of the series. Those events have more detail, more dialogue, and more insight into the characters in Book 1 than they will have in Book 2. I would recommend reading *Unprepared* before reading *Second Chances*. I hope you enjoy the books, and thank you for reading.

A. K. Gentry

LIST OF CHARACTERS
Second Chances, Forewarned Series Book 2

<u>REED FAMILY</u>
Garrett Reed: Wife, Barbara.
Twin sons, Adam and Brett age 14;
Daughter, Riley age 7

Mark Reed: Wife, Ceely.
Son, Caleb age 10;
Daughter, Haley age 5

Ginny Reed: Single
Brad Reed: Single

<u>MARK'S ARMY FRIENDS</u>
Pete Flinn: Single
Alex Freeman: Wife, Erica

Pete's Friends: Max Benton and
Sharon Ingram

<u>DICKSON FAMILY</u> (Friends of Garrett Reed)
Robert Dickson: Wife, Leah.
Son, Michael age 14
Son, Bobby age 10;
Daughter, Geeta age 6

SECOND CHANCES

<u>JOHNSON FAMILY</u> (Neighbors of Ginny Reed)
Aaron Johnson: Wife, Donna.
Son, Carson age 16;
Daughter, Bonnie age 14

Grace Hobson, Donna's sister:
Daughter, Hannah age 14

Tina Koontz: friend of Grace Hobson

<u>YOUNG FAMILY</u> (Related to Ceely Reed)
Mike Young, Ceely's brother: Wife, Heather.
Son, Jackson age 2

Bennett Grimes, Heather's brother: Single

<u>SMITH FAMILY</u> (Neighbors of Ginny Reed)
Rob Smith: Wife, Sarah.
Daughter, Amanda age 14;
Son, Robbie age 10

Marley Bost: Husband, Jack.
Daughter, Abby age 8

<u>SUTTON FAMILY</u> (Neighbors of Ginny Reed)
Tom Sutton: Wife Deceased.
Son, Jerry age 19
Son, Brady age 14

<u>MEYERS FAMILY</u> (Friends of Ginny Reed)
Jacque Meyers: Single
Daughter, Melanie Barefoot age 16

<u>SPEAKS FAMILY</u> (Neighbors of Ginny Reed)
Daniel Speaks: Wife, Janie
Blake Stevens: Brother to Janie

<u>MILLER FAMILY</u> (Neighbors of Ginny Reed)
Hank Miller: Wife, Lacy.
Son, Thomas age 10;
Daughter, Jordan age 7

<u>WASHINGTON, DC</u>
President: Douglas Massey
Secretary of Defense: Donald Evans
National Security Advisor: Jacob Miller
National Security Advisor Aide: Greg Becker

<u>THE COMMITTEE</u>
John Rosen: Wife, Carol
George Thomas

CHAPTER 1

APRIL 5

North Carolina, USA

Brad Reed, tall, strong and tanned from years of farming, stood at a second story window in the house where he had lived his entire life. But never in his wildest imaginings had he ever thought he would have to fight to defend this home with his life.

The motorcycle gang rolled into the drive and pulled up to the large game fence that encircled the house and farm buildings. The United States had been attacked and was now collapsing. The fence had been built to keep deer out of the garden and wild dogs out of the yard, but it wouldn't slow a determined gang.

Brad's jaw tightened as he watched them gather. They wanted his sister, Ginny. She was the only veterinarian in the area who had a reputation for treating large animals and making house calls. The gang had already been there once trying to force her to go with them. That was when Brad and his family learned the bikers had started a compound several miles away, complete with cattle, horses, and fields. Something must have gone terribly wrong if they were willing to risk their lives to take a woman by force.

Mark and Garrett, Brad's older brothers, were stationed at other windows in the house along with some of their friends who were staying with them until the cities became safer. Mark's two army buddies had helped draw up a defensive plan after the gang's first visit. All they could do now was hope that it would hold.

The leader of the group got off his motorcycle and swaggered arrogantly to the fence. Even from his place in the house, Brad could see the grease in his long dark hair. The man wore dirty jeans and a black leather vest with no shirt underneath. His rounded abdomen folded over his belt like a blob. A tattoo of a dagger dripping with blood covered his right upper arm. Behind him, the bikers cut off their engines, and the afternoon grew eerily quiet. So quiet, cows could be heard mooing in the pastures. Brad drew in a slow breath, forcing his pulse to settle.

"We want the doc!" the leader yelled, his voice echoing through the yard. "Give us the doc, and we'll go away. No one has to get hurt."

Mark answered through a bullhorn. "No. She's not going with you. Go away, and no one will get hurt."

"Have it your way," the gang leader called back, a malicious grin spreading across his face. "But don't say we didn't warn you."

He tilted his head and signaled one of his men. The leader watched the house as another biker ran forward with bolt cutters and began slicing a hole in the woven wire.

When the gap was large enough, the leader turned to his group.

"Come on fellas, this is going to be fun."

The first wave of bikers poured through the gap in the wire while others opened fire on the house. He heard Mark shout from downstairs.

"Pick your targets and take them down."

A sudden flash lit the yard, followed by an explosion. Mark's friend, Alex, had the remote control in the other room upstairs and had detonated homemade incendiary bombs. Burning oil and gasoline descended upon the bikers and their machines. The sight and sounds of men burning made Brad's stomach churn.

A loud snap sounded, and a stout tripwire sprang forward with brutal force, catching the bikers closest to the fence. Two men went down instantly and three others were severely wounded. One man's head head rolled across the grass until it thudded into the fence, and Brad gagged.

The bikers faltered, momentarily stunned by their losses, but they quickly regrouped and stormed into the yard, running for the house. Brad steadied his rifle, picked a target and fired. A man dropped, but there was no time for remorse. He shot again. And again. More bodies hit the ground as he heard glass windows shatter and bullets hit the siding.

The gang's numbers began to thin under the coordinated fire from the house and surrounding buildings. For the first time, Brad felt a flicker of hope, that they might hold the line and keep Ginny safe.

Then a woman screamed.

It was Ginny.

The sound tore through him. Every instinct told him to run to her, but he forced himself to stay at the window. Mark and Garrett were downstairs. He had to trust that they would protect her. Too many bikers were still pouring through the fence for him to abandon his post.

Gunfire echoed through the downstairs. Ginny screamed again.

Brad's heart hammered as dread surged through him, but he held his position, praying they would all stay safe.

CHAPTER 2
APRIL 5

North Carolina, USA

Brad jolted up in bed, chest heaving. A light sheen of sweat covered his face and chest. He looked around, trying to shake the fogginess from his brain. It was dark and quiet. There was no gunfire, no shouting. He breathed a deep sigh of relief. Just a dream.

Brad jumped in surprise when a scream shattered the quiet. That was Ginny. This was real.

He grabbed the baseball bat leaning against the night stand and sprinted down the hall. He pushed Ginny's door open and rushed inside. Ginny thrashed under tangled sheets as she screamed again.

Brad reached her side and gently shook her shoulders.

"Ginny, wake up. You're having a nightmare."

Ginny sat straight up in the bed, eyes wide and alert.

"Brad?" she asked, running a hand through her knotted hair. "Are you okay? Where's everybody else?"

"Ginny, you had a nightmare. No one else is here. It's just you and me."

Ginny looked around. The dim, predawn light barely showed the contents of her room. Her alarm clock glowed 6:00 am. She was alone. No one was sharing her room. There was no gunfire.

"Thank goodness," she said, pushing her hair back. "That was the most vivid dream I've ever had. It felt like I was actually there."

"I know what you mean. Mine was the same way."

"There must have been something wrong with supper last night," Ginny said. "Maybe a hallucinatory fungus was in the salad or salad dressing." She threw back the covers. "Well, I can't go back to sleep. I'm going to get dressed and make coffee. Want some?"

"Definitely. Maybe we should compare dreams."

By 6:30, they sat in the breakfast nook, hands wrapped around steaming mugs of coffee, both still shaken.

"What was your dream about?" Ginny asked.

"The end of the world apocalypse. Literally."

"Sounds like mine," Ginny replied. "Tell me about it."

"I was on the tractor planting corn," Brad said. "My phone rang, and it was Mark. He told me that North Korea had fired a nuclear missile toward us, but it detonated over the Pacific. He wanted to bring his family here. He said things were going to get bad. He told me he'd talked to you and that you were on the way home with two of his Army buddies."

Ginny's eyes widened.

"Brad, that's exactly what happened in my dream! I was in the airport about to go to St. Louis on the Pure Pet trip to talk about my supplements when all the flights were cancelled. Two guys in the airport lounge were talking about Mark because they had all served in Afghanistan together. Mark told me to bring them here."

"Alex and Pete?" Brad asked.

"Yes!" Ginny said incredulously. "Brad, why would we have the same dream? Did yours end in a gunfight with a motorcycle gang?"

"In my dream, I was stationed at an upstairs window," he said.

"Then I heard you screaming. What happened in your dream?"

"One of the gang members got into the house through the back door." Her breath hitched. "I was struggling to get away from him. Pete heard the noise and came out of his room. The biker raised his gun and shot at Pete. I don't know if he hit Pete because you woke me up."

Brad sipped his coffee and quietly studied Ginny. Her blue eyes and dark-blonde hair matched the other Reed siblings except for Garrett, whose hair had turned prematurely gray. Brad stood over six feet tall, lean and muscular. Ginny, tall herself, had her hair pull back in the classic ponytail she usually treaded through a ball cap.

"So, the dreams match," Brad said, gripping his mug. "But we each experienced different parts."

"Why would we dream the same thing?" Ginny asked. "Do you think we should take it seriously?"

"I think we should take it very seriously," Brad said, his voice steady. "The Bible says that men will dream dreams. I think this is a warning."

"What should we do?" she asked. "Should we go ahead and get the supplies that were hard to find in the dream?"

"Yes, and I'm suddenly glad my purchase of the Thompson farm next door is complete. Let's make lists. You handle medical supplies and food. I'll take farm supplies, garden seeds and defense. Then we can tackle the rest together."

"All right," Ginny said. "I remember needing medical supplies for humans in the dream. I'll order a bunch from my supplier. If none of this happens, I can still use them at the clinic or in my truck."

Ginny was a veterinarian with a PhD in animal nutrition. Her supplement line had become very successful. Brad, trained as a chemist, managed the plant that manufactured it.

"I want to close the plant Monday," Ginny said. "I'll give the employees a day off with pay. They won't complain, and they deserve it."

I'll take care of the plant," Brad said. "I'll move all the extra supplements here. We can use them for our animals. If nothing happens, we can return them. And I'll make sure the building is secure. One of the guys can help me with that Friday."

Brad's phone rang. It was their brother Mark.

"Hey, Mark," Brad said. "What's up?"

"Brad," Mark said, "this is going to sound crazy, but I had the worst dream last night. It really affected me. I want to stash some supplies there so I can bring the family. I really feel like something bad is about to happen. I'm probably overreacting, but I can't shake it."

Brad glanced at Ginny.

"Mark, I'm going to put you on speaker."

Brad placed his phone on the table.

"Ginny and I had the same dream last night," Brad said, "and it was disturbing."

"In your dream, were we attacked by North Korea and terrorists, and the country fell apart?" Mark asked.

"Pretty much," Brad said. "My dream and Ginny's ended in a gunfight with a motorcycle gang. How did yours end?"

"Brad," Mark said, "I woke up shooting at men in the front yard and hearing Ginny scream in the kitchen."

Brad and Ginny stared at each other, stunned.

Ginny's phone rang. It was their other brother, Garrett.

"Hey, Garrett," she said. "How are you?"

"Ginny, I had the worst dream last night, and I can't shake it," Garrett said. "Can I bring some supplies and put them in the basement? I know it sounds strange, but I feel like I need to do this to prepare for something."

"Garrett," she said, looking at Brad with wide eyes, "Brad's here with Mark on his phone. I'm switching these calls to video."

Ginny made the connections, then she and Brad sat together, watching their brothers on the screen.

"Now, that's better," she said.

"Garrett," Ginny said, "Mark, Brad and I, had the very same dream last night. Tell us about yours."

"North Korea launched missiles at us, and terrorists attacked," Garrett said. "Travel stopped, shortages took place, and we were all at the farm trying to survive."

"That's exactly what Brad and I dreamed," Ginny said. "Mark did too. We're taking this seriously."

"I have classes to teach," Mark said, "but I'm free after three. Garrett, when can you get away today?"

"I have to represent some clients in court this morning, but I'm free after lunch," Garrett told them.

"I think that Garrett and I should come to the farm this afternoon," Mark said. "We can plan together."

"That sounds good," Brad said. "We still have to work, too, but we'll start prepping."

"Come as soon as you can," Ginny said. With that plan made, the phone calls ended.

Brad sighed and rubbed his face.

"It's barely seven in the morning. Why do I feel like I need a stiff drink?"

"I understand," Ginny said, nodding. "Today is Wednesday. We have five days to get ready, and I'm sure I won't relax until I go to the airport on April 10 and none of the dream comes true."

"I'm going to go see the Thompsons," Brad said, standing. "Since I bought their farm, they planned to slowly move to their son's house. I want to encourage them to move sooner. I hope they'll understand."

"They will," Ginny said. "They're believers. They'll take this seriously. But, I agree, they need to be in a safe place if this all comes about. Maybe they can just get ready and wait until April 10th to actually make the move."

"When I get back, I'm going to plant corn," Brad said. "No matter what happens, that still needs to be done. I won't get it finished, but if I start it now, we'll have time to refill the gasoline tanks on Friday."

"Good thinking," Ginny said. She checked her watch. "I still need to open the clinic this morning. Thank goodness we're closed this afternoon."

CHAPTER 3

APRIL 5

North Carolina, USA

Ginny and Brad went about their jobs, but every free minute was taken up with adding more items to the supply and to-do lists they were making. Early in the afternoon they both came into the house for lunch and to get ready for their brothers' arrival.

Ginny decided to walk around the house and think about changes she could make to accommodate the number of people that would soon be living there. She had inherited the house, outbuildings and some land from her parents. Gradually, she bought the rest of the farmland from her brothers.

The original part of the house had been built in the early 1800s. The front was two stories with symmetrical rooms and four chimneys. Two bedrooms and a bath were upstairs. Downstairs held a parlor, sitting room, bathroom, and a large dining room which opened into a den. The newer addition extended off the back with a reverse gable and housed the kitchen, office, den, bathrooms, bedrooms, and a basement.

With a pad and pencil in her hands, Ginny surveyed the bedrooms and made notes on items that they might need to make life with an overflowing household easier. With that task completed, Ginny took a carbonated drink from the refrigerator and sat on the couch in the den next to the kitchen. A wave of doubt washed over her. Were they crazy? Who drops everything and reacts to a dream like it's a real warning? The Reed siblings just did.

She stood as Brad came into the kitchen and got his own carbonated drink from the refrigerator.

"We need to make sure we stock up on drinks and coffee," he said, taking a long drink of the cold beverage.

"Lots of coffee," Ginny agreed.

They had just laid their completed lists on the dining room table when Garrett strode through the back door and pulled them into a hug.

"I don't know what to say or where to start," he said, eyeing the papers on the table. "But I firmly believe we have been given a vision of the future, a prophecy, and we should take it seriously."

"Have a seat," Ginny said, retrieving a glass of iced tea for him. "You can look over the lists that Brad and I have been working on all morning."

"This is fascinating," Garrett said as he read. "I made lists, too, but they're nothing like yours. I was led to think about different things."

Garrett pulled several sheets of paper from his back pocket and spread them across the table. His handwriting filled each page. Ginny scanned them, surprised.

"This is amazing," Ginny said. "I never would've thought of half of this. Your dream must have had your own experiences woven into it as well as the parts we all shared. That's what Brad and I noticed."

I rearranged my appointments to have my afternoons free," Garrett said. "And I'm taking Friday off to have a long weekend to get ready."

The screen door banged when Mark walked in. He hugged each of them in turn.

"Are we crazy?" Mark asked looking from one sibling to the next. "Do we have some type of mental telepathy, or have we just had a vision?"

"I think we've had a vision," Garrett said. "No matter what we call it, we need to follow up on it. Everything we do over the next four days could affect the rest of our lives. We need to survive, but we also need to show God's love and be a blessing to others who will not have had a chance to prepare."

The others agreed.

"That said," continued Garrett, "Let's start this meeting with prayer." The four held hands while Garrett thanked God for his blessings then asked for His guidance, wisdom and protection.

Settling around the table, they discovered that Mark had an entirely different set of items that he thought they needed to get for the farm, all scrawled out on a piece of notebook paper. The four were amazed, but not surprised, that each of them had been led to focus on different preparations. By the end of the evening, they had formulated a plan.

Brad took the responsibility to make sure the farm had everything it would need for the garden and crops. Ginny volunteered for medical supplies, household items, and cleaning supplies. Mark took weapons, ammunition and outdoor survival supplies. Garrett took solar power, electronics, extra supplies for generators, and lighting supplies for power outages.

Ginny added perishable foods and food preservation supplies to her list. Brad, Mark, and Garrett divided nonperishable food items to be bought from long term supply websites, with everything set to be overnighted to the farm. Everyone would get paper supplies, toiletries, special foods their families would want, and recreational items such as yard games, cards, and board games. They agreed that surviving needed to include joy.

The group continued their discussion over dinner.

"In your dreams, did any of you have the feeling that there were other people involved, but they weren't revealed?" Ginny asked. "I felt like there were shadows of people moving in and out behind the scenes. I think that's because I really want Jacque here."

"Yes," Garrett answered. "I just thought they were people who would come later or pass through. I don't think anything we saw is completely written in stone. I believe we have the chance to change things for the better."

After dinner, Garrett ended the meeting with prayer. They agreed to meet the next night remotely with a computer program Garrett used for online meetings. They would compare notes and finalize last-minute plans.

When Mark and Garrett left, Brad grabbed his jacket.

"I'm going to see Holly. I want to talk to her about coming to stay here."

"Good idea," Ginny said. "I'm tired, so I'll see you in the morning."

The screen door slammed behind him, and soon Ginny heard his truck rumble down the drive. She got her phone and texted her best friend, Jacque Meyers, an emergency room physician in High Point and the closest thing to a true sister that Ginny had. Ginny wanted her here.

Brad had been dating Holly Baker for two years. He planned to ask her to marry him, but he had never settled on a romantic way to propose. Tonight, he knew, would be the least romantic proposal in history.

Holly stood at a window watching Brad's truck pull into her driveway. He got out of his truck and walked to the house. She opened the door before he reached it and hugged him.

"What's going on?" she asked as she closed the door behind him. "You sounded nervous on the phone. Is everything okay?"

Brad took her hand and led her to the couch.

"Let's sit down," he said. "I need to talk to you."

Once they were seated, Brad took a deep breath.

"I'm afraid you're not going to believe me, but I need you to hear me out before you say anything." He met her eyes. "Last night I had a very vivid dream. When I woke up, I thought I had been fighting a motorcycle gang in our front yard and Ginny was screaming in the kitchen.

"It took me a moment to realize it was a dream, but Ginny was really screaming. She was having a nightmare. When I woke her up, she was confused. She had been dreaming about a gunfight with a motorcycle gang at the house. We compared details and discovered we had the exact same dream."

He continued, "This morning, while we were talking about it, both Mark and Garrett called. They had the same dream. Holly, I really think we've been given a vision of what's coming. I know this isn't how you pictured this happening, but I came here tonight because I want you to marry me this week and move to the farm where you'll be safe."

"Marry you this week?" Holly asked incredulously. She stared at him. "I can't do that, Brad. Even if I thought we were ready for marriage, I want the big deal, not a hasty ceremony in town hall or a preacher's office."

"Holly, please," he said, tightening his grip on her hand. "This is serious. The four of us are working like crazy to get supplies put away before everything happens."

"I don't understand the rush. What do you believe is going to happen?"

"We're going to be attacked with bombs and tactical weapons by North Korea and terrorists," he said. "There will be supply shortages everywhere, and then our economy will collapse."

Holly blinked then laughed. She ran her hand through her hair and shifted on the couch.

"Brad, you all saw the same news report. The commentators were trying to scare people to boost their ratings. Nothing's going to happen. We live in America, Brad. That stuff may happen in other countries, but not in ours."

"You're wrong, Holly," he said. "It can happen here, and it's going to. I've seen it."

"You haven't seen anything, Brad," Holly said, dropping his hand. "And I'm not going to marry you. You're talking crazy. I don't believe you had a vision. And even if something did happen, I'm not spending my apocalypse with a bunch of crazy Bible-thumping kooks."

Brad felt as if she'd thrown ice water in his face. How had he misjudged her so badly? He thought she loved him enough to trust him. Heat rose in his checks, anger rising at the way she had spoken about him and his family.

"Okay, Holly," he said, his voice tightening. "If none of this happens, you can call me the crazy kook that I am. But if it does happen, you've lost your chance. Don't come knocking on my door expecting me to take you in and keep you safe."

"Don't worry," Holly snapped. "I'll take my chances here. I doubt there would be any fun at your place anyway. It would be all work and Bible study. No thanks."

Brad stared at her, stunned. Without another word he stood and walked out the door, slamming it hard enough to rattle the window next to it. He stormed to the driveway, got into his truck and sat for a moment trying to understand what had just happened.

The woman he loved had just rejected his proposal and mocked his family and faith. Maybe in time he would realize that he had avoided a bad mistake, but tonight he just felt the crushing weight of loss. Brad felt like a tight band was squeezing his chest as he started the truck and drove back to the farm.

The house was dark except for a light over the kitchen sink. Brad was glad Ginny had gone to bed. He didn't want to talk with her or anyone. He climbed the stairs to his room, got ready for bed, and finally laid down. A single tear escaped before he could stop it.

He brushed it away angrily. He would not grieve for a woman who callously dismissed his affection and attempts to keep her safe. Brad turned on his side to go to sleep, but sleep was slow in coming. Holly's refusal and insults kept replaying in his mind. Finally, well after midnight, exhaustion took over and Brad slept.

CHAPTER 4

APRIL 6

Cayman Islands

John Rosen and George Thomas had been best friends since they met in the foster care system of Chicago. At nine years old, they had been taken from their families and placed in the large group home on the outskirts of the city. They had been the youngest in the house, which had been a distinct disadvantage. John and George learned that to survive, they would have to look out for each other.

Life in the home had been hard and sometimes dangerous. By the time they finished middle school, John and George had become hardened survivors. They could manipulate their housemates and schoolmates without intimidation, but everyone understood the two would easily resort to violence over a perceived slight or threat.

Earning money became their driving force. As soon as they could legally obtain jobs, they worked after school, opened bank accounts, and began investing. Almost as important as money to them was power. They vowed to work together to never feel poor or powerless again. Through their struggles, they began to hate their living situation and Chicago in general. Chicago became the face and the name of their misery.

Now in their forties, the friends had amassed a fortune through hard work and wise investments. Those investments were used to buy struggling companies and turn them into successful empires, but that was the legal face of their business. The companies John and George bought were used to launder money and build bank accounts in Switzerland and the Cayman Islands. Their investments included real estate in the United States, Switzerland, Crete, Greece, and the Cayman Islands.

That morning, John and George sat at the dining room table of their home that sat on a large chunk of coastline in a remote corner of the Cayman's. They ate their normal breakfast of eggs and fruit while they looked out across the white sand at the blue water. John looked around to make sure none of the staff were nearby.

"Everything has fallen into place quite well, don't you think?" he asked George, taking a sip of his coffee.

"No one will see this coming," George replied, smiling. "Our group has worked hard. We've been quiet, diligent, and determined to play the long game. Your idea to keep the different factions and cells isolated has been brilliant. No one knows the whole picture except for us. Well, us and Carol."

Carol Rosen was John's wife of twenty years. She had been raised in the group home in Chicago alongside John and George, and her hatred of the city and its system was as strong as theirs.

"Yes," John said nodding. "She and the kids are safe back in the states. We want the kids to be completely innocent in all this. They aren't in any of the target areas, but they also have a large bunker and resources just in case."

"Good," George replied. He had never married, but he was emotionally invested in John's family. He liked being the 'fun uncle' for the kids.

John looked at his watch.

"We'd better get going. I dread the long flight to Davos, but we need to get there a few days before the meeting this weekend. We have a lot to get finalized before Monday."

The men stood and carried their dirty dishes to the kitchen. The house was full of staff, but the habits instilled in the group home never left them.

Damien — the estate's groundskeeper, maintenance man, and driver — took John and George to the private airport a mile from the house. The two pilots were already there and had everything ready to go. John and George boarded the private jet, sat in the plush chairs and buckled their seatbelts. Within ten minutes they were climbing through the clouds to cruising altitude. As soon as the plane leveled, they would move to a conference table and get to work.

⸺◆O◆⸺

North Carolina, USA

Brad drove into Elkin to get to the farming co-op as soon as it opened. He filled his truck with fertilizer, seeds, lime, herbicides, insecticides, dog food, chicken feed, and supplemental cattle feed. He dropped that load at the farm then arranged for the farm's gasoline and propane tanks to be filled on Friday.

After planting another field of corn, Brad checked the service records on the large farm equipment. By late afternoon, he was back in town buying replacement parts, fence posts, rolls of tall game fencing, rolls of barbed wire fencing, multiple pairs of work gloves in all sizes, and two of every hand tool he could find.

After clinic hours, Ginny went into Elkin to get as many toiletries, paper products, garbage bags, duct tape, feminine supplies, and over the counter medications as her truck could hold. She went to a home improvement store and bought an upright freezer to be delivered the next morning. On a second trip she purchased linens, cleaning supplies, lanterns, lantern oil, and a corn hole game. Knowing she and Brad would be tired, she ordered take-out barbeque from their favorite restaurant for dinner.

During the remote conference meeting later that evening, the four siblings compared items purchased and other things to be considered. Garrett and Mark planned to bring their first load of supplies the next afternoon. It was April 6, and they were all feeling the stress of time running out.

CHAPTER 5

APRIL 7

North Carolina, USA

Ginny left the clinic long enough to receive and install the freezer when it arrived at the house. She plugged it in and left it empty to begin cooling. Along with the freezer, Ginny bought a smaller refrigerator to store the medications she had ordered that needed to be kept cold, and she put that unit in her bedroom.

When Ginny stepped back outside, she found Brad watching the delivery man filling up the propane tanks. She gave him a thumbs up before getting back into her work truck and returning to the clinic.

After the clinic closed at 1:00 pm, Ginny drove to the grocery store and loaded her cart with bacon, ham, sausage, hotdogs, hamburger, chicken and beef. She took everything home and packed it in the freezer. Once she saw how much space remained, she estimated how much more she could buy and decided to fill the unit up completely.

Late in the afternoon Ginny and Brad watched an unfamiliar F250 pickup pulling a camper up the driveway. They realized it was Mark. He told them that he had traded his SUV for the truck then went to the large RV dealer outside Winston-Salem. He bought the camper to put on one of the two RV sites their parents had installed in the backyard.

Once the trailer was in position, Mark opened it to show a large supply of ammunition, cases of gun cleaning supplies, and a few extra firearms. The three turned around when they heard another engine and saw Garrett's SUV pulling an enclosed trailer. His vehicle was filled to the brim with luggage and supplies. When he opened the trailer, they saw an electric golf cart as well as two large marine batteries with converters and solar panels.

"I thought the golf cart would be a quiet way to get around the farm," Garrett said. He hesitated. "I finally talked with my friend, Robert Dickson. He admitted he'd had a very limited dream like ours and a sense of foreboding. He called and asked if he could come to the farm. I told him yes, that he had been in our dreams as well. I think he was relieved. I even offered to bring a load of his things over this weekend. I feel bad that I didn't think to call him sooner."

"I had a similar conversation with my brother-in-law, Mike Young," Mark said. "They're preparing and will come if everything happens the way we've seen. He's a contractor, so he'll have all of his tools. His brother-in-law, Bennett, is coming with him, just like in the dream. He said Bennett plans on getting some very interesting supplies from the outdoor store where he works."

Ginny listened to the conversation. In the dream she had been annoyed with Mark for inviting so many people to the farm, but now it seemed that each person had a purpose for being there.

Brad reported that all the propane and gasoline tanks on the farm had been filled that day. Also, he had closed the supplement plant and placed the inventory in the equipment shed. Then, he and Ginny helped their brothers unload their vehicles.

"I don't know if this means anything, but the stock market has been very volatile this afternoon," Garrett said when they had finished. "It closed down almost 3,000 points, and it's Friday. Who knows what

Monday morning will bring."

"I got out of the market yesterday," Mark said, checking a stock app on his phone. "Maybe we weren't the only ones with dreams. It could be others are trying to hedge their bets before everything falls apart." The others agreed, admitting they had made financial changes as well.

"Mark, have you contacted your army friends?" Brad asked.

"No," Mark said after a pause. "For some reason I felt that I shouldn't. I think they're the ones who are supposed to prove to us that this is real. If they're at the airport and Ginny connects with them, then we know everything will take place as we saw in the vision. Remember, she met them before we found out what happened."

"All right," Brad said. "You have to follow what you think you've been led to do."

"Today is April 7th," Mark said. "We only have two days left to get finished. I plan to make multiple trips back and forth bringing things in. Let's plan to stop everything Sunday afternoon to discuss what we've done and what we may be able to manage on Monday if things happen as foreseen."

Everyone agreed.

After Mark and Garrett left, Brad and Ginny went to Elkin for a quick supper and another run to the large discount store. Ginny bought cheese, deli meats, and butter to add to the new freezer. Both she and Brad picked up extra work clothes and underwear. By the time the store closed, they had filled the truck bed with three carts worth of merchandise.

When they got home Ginny said, 'I'll put the perishables in the freezer. The rest can wait until tomorrow. I'm beat."

"Agreed," Brad said. "I'm tired, too."

Switzerland

John was exhausted. He hadn't slept on the long flight from the Cayman's, and they'd been working nonstop since they got to Davos. A dull ache was settling behind his eyes.

"Well," he said to George as the door closed on their last interviewee. "What do you think?" They had spent the afternoon interviewing candidates for the final staff positions they needed.

"Alice in HR did a good job searching them out," George said. "They're just like us. No family, angry at the system, eager and driven. Only a decade or more younger than we are and brilliant with today's technology. Plus, not a one argued about the nondisclosure agreement they had to sign just to get an interview. They're all suitable. We only need four, but let's hire all five. It will lighten the current workload, which I'm sure will actually increase in a few days."

"Agreed," John said. "Let's notify them and get them settled in the company housing apartments. Tomorrow, we need to have a staff meeting for all of the Davos employees."

"I can arrange that," George said. "We'll do it over lunch. Before that, I'll touch base with all the regional managers individually and make sure they have the correct timeline of events."

"Are the warehouses in Argentina at capacity?" John asked. "Once this is over, we're going to need to rebuild a lot of infrastructure."

"They're full, and we're still manufacturing electrical transformers, computer chips, and steel," George said.

"Good," John said, yawning. "I'm going to bed. I need to be up early. I have meetings with a few CEO's of the legit businesses in the morning. I'll see you tomorrow."

John left the office to go to their chalet. George planned to work a little longer, then he would head back and turn in for the night as well.

CHAPTER 6

APRIL 8

North Carolina, USA

Ginny woke early on Saturday morning. She sat at the kitchen island sipping coffee, mentally going over the bedrooms and where to place everyone if their dreams turned out to be real.

Mark's wife, Ceely, was a physical therapist. She had worked with Mark while he was at Walter Reed Hospital after he was wounded in Afghanistan. They fell in love and got married. Ginny would place them in the upstairs bedroom that had been Mark's while growing up. He still preferred it. Their ten-year-old son, Caleb, would stay downstairs with the other boys in the bunkroom, and their five-year-old daughter, Haley, would sleep with the other girls.

In her dream, the little girls, Haley, Riley, and Geeta had slept in the basement on air mattresses. Ginny decided to turn the last small room upstairs in the old part of the house into their bedroom. Over the years, it had become a storage space, so she would move everything to the attic before the others arrived. The girls could sleep on air mattresses in that room instead of the basement, which would be completely dark if the power went out.

If everything unfolded as shown in the vision, she would put Mark's friend, Alex and his wife Erica, in the other bedroom in the front of the old house. They would all share the bathroom that had been converted from a bedroom when Ginny and her brothers were growing up. Ginny smiled; she bet no other bathroom in the state had a fireplace or as much storage space as the two bathrooms in the old house.

Brad already planned to move to the office so Robert and Leah Dickson could have his room. Leah had been working in Northern Virginia when she met Robert. They married and moved to Winston-Salem where Robert worked as an engineer. Leah was now a homemaker. Her calm demeanor and kindness managed to soothe many tense situations. Their sons, fourteen-year-old Michael and ten-year-old Bobby, would stay in the bunkroom in the basement. Their daughter, Geeta, age six, would sleep on the air mattresses with Haley and Riley in the emptied storage room upstairs.

That left the last spare bedroom in the addition for Garrett and Barbara. Barbara, also a homemaker, and had to be the most organized person Ginny knew. Their twin sons, Adam and Brett, age fourteen, would stay in the bunkroom, and daughter Riley, age 7, would sleep on the air mattresses with Haley and Geeta.

If Pete came like in the dream, he could stay in the sitting room which would be converted into a bedroom. Ceely's brother, Mike, and his family would stay in the RV. That left Bennett. She needed to talk with Mark about Bennett. She knew he wouldn't want to stay with Mike's family, but there was no comfortable place left.

Still sitting at the kitchen island clinging to the last warmth in her cup of coffee, Ginny watched Brad enter the room and fix a bowl of cereal. He had been subdued for the last couple days. She had assumed it was the stress of all the preparations, but now she wasn't so sure.

"Brad, are you all right?" she asked. "You haven't been your usual optimistic self. Is anything wrong?"

Brad sighed and sat beside Ginny.

"I asked Holly to marry me this week and move here," he said, solemnly, pushing the cereal around the bowl with his spoon. "I told her about the dreams and our preparations. She didn't believe me. In fact, she thought I was out of my mind and broke things off with me."

Ginny was not expecting that.

"Oh, Brad, I'm so sorry," she said, her brows furrowed with concern. "That had to be hurtful. I understand your wanting privacy, but you could have told us so we could support you."

"I know, Ginny," he said, looking down and stirring his cereal. "But I just wasn't ready to talk about it. I really loved her, and I hate I misjudged her so badly. I thought we saw things the same way. I couldn't have been more wrong."

Brad ducked his head, his eyes filling with something like shame before he continued.

"I'm afraid I said something terrible in the moment of hurt and anger. I told her that if none of this happened, she could call me the crazy kook she thought I was. But if it happened as we had seen in the vision, then she had missed her opportunity and not to come knocking on my door."

"How could anything be less Christian than that?" he asked sadly, shaking his head. "That's what I feel the worst about. I think God has allowed me to dodge the bullet of a bad mistake, but I could have handled it better."

"What did she say?" Ginny asked.

"Holly said to not worry. She wouldn't be interested in joining a bunch of Bible-thumping kooks, anyway. So, I guess it's all for the best."

"I agree that you're right in thinking you narrowly missed making a mistake," Ginny said as she placed a hand on his arm. "I would have hated to see you miserable in a mismatched marriage."

"Thanks," Brad said, patting her hand. "There's no need to tell everyone. You're the only one who knew I was dating her."

"You're right," Ginny said. "There's no need to talk about it to anyone else. But if you need to vent, remember that I'm here, and I have a surprisingly strong shoulder for a skinny veterinarian."

"A goofy veterinarian," Brad teased with a faint grin. He ate a spoonful of cereal before changing the subject. "Are we going into town together or do you want to go separately?"

"I feel separate will be more efficient. We have different places to go and different things to get. Plus, we'll be able to get more supplies if we have both trucks." Ginny looked at her watch. "It's time for the stores to open. I need to get going."

"You're going to be okay, you know," Ginny said as she looked at Brad. "God looked out for you. He will send you the perfect mate in His time."

"I know," Brad said. "I think it's now more embarrassing than hurtful. How could I read someone so wrong?" He sighed. "I need to finish this cereal and get going, too."

"Do you know when Mark and Garrett are coming?" she asked.

"No. But they can unload and make several trips even if we aren't here," Brad replied then put a spoonful of cereal into his mouth.

Ginny put her most comfortable ball cap on and pulled her ponytail through the back opening.

"I'm off." Ginny waved on her way out the door. "See ya."

Brad chuckled and turned back to his breakfast. She had a way of lifting his spirits. She always had.

On the way to Elkin, Ginny saw a furniture store. On impulse, she turned into the parking lot then went inside. Thirty minutes later, Ginny had bought two sets of bunk beds with mattresses. She would put them in the storage room upstairs for the little girls instead of using air mattresses. She didn't know why she hadn't done this before for family gatherings. The manager of the store promised to have the beds delivered that afternoon.

Brad was tired. After eating a quick sandwich for lunch, he unloaded the last of the lumber supplies he bought for the construction projects that were planned as well as extras to have on hand. He looked at the supply, then at his bank account. Money wasn't limitless, but if everything fell apart, it would be a long time before treated lumber would be available again.

Thinking about lumber shortages, Brad decided to go by Bob Smith's farm. Bob had a sawmill on his property. He would ask if it was still in operation and quietly suggest Bob get it in good working order and get spare parts. He would have to explain why, but he would just take the chance that Bob would understand. Bob and his family sat two rows behind them in church every Sunday. Maybe he had a dream, too.

Bob Smith's farmhouse sat back off the road behind a stand of trees. Brad pulled up to the front of the house and got out. Doris, Bob's wife, was out front weeding the flower bed.

"Hey, Brad," she called. "What brings you out here?"

"Is Bob around?" Brad asked.

"Yes," Doris said. "He's in the barn. Go on back."

"Thanks." Brad walked back to the barn.

Bob saw him coming and walked out to meet him.

"Hey, Brad," he said as he extended his hand. "What can I do for you?"

Brad shook his friend's hand.

"I've been thinking about the time I came with Dad when he brought a truck of logs to your sawmill. Is it still in working order?"

Bob gave him a curious look.

"Well, funny you should mention it. I've been checking it out over the last few days, because it hasn't been used in a while. I took it apart, cleaned and oiled the parts, and put it back together. I even ordered some replacement parts that should be here tomorrow. Why do you ask?" Bob watched Brad carefully.

"I was just wondering," Brad said, leaning against the barn door. "I had a feeling we might be needing your services in the future, and I thought I would ask you about it."

"Got a feeling?" Bob asked, his eyebrows raised and giving Brad a knowing look. "You mean maybe you had a dream?"

"You too?" Brad asked incredulously, suddenly standing up straight.

"Yep," Bob said. "I wondered if anyone else had one. Can you tell me about it? How detailed was yours?"

"Pretty damn real, Bob," Brad answered, running a hand nervously through his hair. "We wound up with a lot of people at the farm, and I woke up during a gun battle with a motorcycle gang."

"Whew," Bob said. "That's worse than mine. I was just having trouble feeding my family. My brother and his family from Charlotte came up in my dream. They barely got here. He's preparing and coming up tomorrow night." Bob pointed to the bins in the back of his pickup. "Doris and I have been cleaning out the shelves in every grocery, pharmacy, and hardware store we can find. I've been planting a bigger garden than we usually have, too. My kids are all planning to get here this evening or tomorrow."

"Garrett, Mark, Ginny, and I all had the dream and have been working like crazy trying to get a feeling of preparedness. But no matter how much we get, I feel like it's still not enough. Ginny will still make house calls if you need her for your horses, Bob. Don't hesitate to call."

"Good to know," Bob said. "When the time comes, bring your logs. The old mill will be working."

Brad shook his friend's hand again.

"Thanks, Bob. I'm glad I stopped by. It's reassuring to know some-one else had the same sort of vision we did." Brad left and continued into Elkin to finish his purchases for the day.

Looking around the basement storage area, Ginny put down her list and secured a pile of bins that looked like it was going to fall. She was tired. She had stuffed supplies in every nook and cranny that she could find in the storage room and her bedroom. She realized she needed to rethink this because the others would need space, too. On her next trip into town, she would buy several more storage bins. Things could be stored in the equipment shed if they were secured. Storing bulky paper products out there or in Garrett's trailer would save space in the house.

She was on her way out the door for one more trip to the grocery store when Mark drove up. He was pulling another travel trailer identical to the first and parked it on the second site. He got out of the truck and walked over to where she stood.

"Hey, Ginny," he said, "I brought another trailer. I had Bennett in mind. I know that in the dreams Aaron's family used the second site, but I got one anyway. We can park a third behind these two and still give them electricity. I also brought supplies to hook other trailers into the septic tank."

"It's fine, Mark," she said. "I'd rather have an extra one than be wishing we had thought of it. I see the dream as a warning, but I also think we can arrange a different outcome. At least I hope so, because I don't want a shootout at the OK Corral in my front yard."

"Me neither," Mark said, rolling his eyes. "I have more supplies. Where do you want them?"

Ginny asked what they were. When Mark answered, she said, "Put them inside. You and Brad can organize those things in the basement. I'd help you, but I'm about to make my last trip into town for the day."

"No worries," he said. "I'll take care of this and be on my way. I still have a lot of things to do, too. I'll put personal things in my usual bedroom and Caleb's things in the bunkroom. Be careful in town."

"Already getting into the mindset, huh," Ginny said with a sad smile. "Today and tomorrow could be the last normal days we will know for a very long time. I want to enjoy the peace and feeling of security that will vanish on Monday. Brad is around here somewhere. The equipment shed, I think. He can help you if you can find him."

Ginny got into her truck, waved, and drove back to Elkin. This trip was all about food, staples, spices, and dairy products. She bought more coffee and a machine to carbonate water in case all those sodas she had went flat.

Going through the last two aisles Ginny passed the candy display. Without thinking twice, she filled her cart with candy. She would hide all of this and bring it out for holidays and special occasions. That gave her another idea. She went back and got marshmallows and graham crackers. Nothing like an evening campfire and smores to lighten the mood.

When Ginny returned home, Mark's truck was gone but Garrett's SUV was parked beside the barn. He and Brad were unloading items into the equipment shed. When they saw her park beside the house, they came up to help her unload her purchases onto the kitchen island.

Brad saw the candy. "I want one of those now!"

Ginny laughed and threw a bag at him.

"Go ahead. I can get more tomorrow," she said.

She laughed when she saw Garrett making a sad face and threw a bag of candy at him, too. He smiled as he opened it and took out a piece of what he called chocolate goodness.

The three heard a large truck coming up the drive and went outside. They helped the delivery men unload the bunk beds and put them in the upstairs storage room. After the truck left, Brad and Garrett helped her assemble the beds.

Ginny brought in rolling carts with drawers and placed them by the beds for the girls to use as makeshift dressers. She made the beds with matching linens and comforters and sighed with approval. Everything was in place.

Switzerland

John Rosen looked at his watch. Everything was following the plan and timeline. He was pleased with the staff meeting. The new employees were integrating well with the veteran staff.

He had just enough time to shower and change before dinner. The members of The Committee, along with the representatives of participating countries, were coming for a meeting. He needed them to be impressed with the wealth and power he would display. There could be no question about who was in control.

CHAPTER 7

APRIL 9

Brad woke early again, before dawn. The stress of getting prepared and the aftermath of Holly's rejection were beginning to affect his sleep. Today was Sunday, the last day they had to get ready. He and Ginny agreed to wait until after the early church service at 8:30 am to resume the hunt for supplies.

They sat through the service and participated, but their hearts were heavy, weighed down by what the dreams had shown. They wanted to warn the others, to plead with them to prepare, but something held them back. They looked at their friends, sitting in the pews, singing, and unaware. Ginny started to cry. Brad squeezed her hand letting her know he knew exactly how she felt. When the last hymn started, which would bring the service to a close, Ginny left. She couldn't stop crying, and she didn't want anyone to ask her why. Brad followed her, his expression mirroring hers. If anyone noticed, neither of them saw it.

Bob and Doris Smith saw Brad and Ginny leave the church. Ginny was crying. Bob took Doris's hand, and they followed the Reeds outside. They approached Brad and Ginny, who had stopped at the edge of the sidewalk while Ginny regained control.

"I know," Doris said, stepping forward and hugging Ginny. "I feel the same way."

Ginny stared at her.

"You had a dream, too?" she asked Doris then looked at Brad.

"Sorry, Ginny," Brad said. "I was going to tell you, but it slipped my mind in the hustle. Bob and I compared notes yesterday afternoon when I went to ask him about his sawmill."

Ginny took a deep ragged breath.

"I'm sorry," she said, looking between her brother and the Smith's. "The service was overwhelming. I wanted to shout to everyone to get ready, but I felt a weight stopping me. It was like God was telling me He had different plans for us all. Why do I feel like we've been given a very special warning with immense responsibility?"

"I don't know, Ginny, but I felt it too," Brad said. The sanctuary doors opened, and a line of church members flooded outside.

"So did we," Bob added, glancing at his watch. "We need to get going. If you need us, don't be afraid to call us."

"Same," Brad said. "We'll need friends and allies if this gets as bad as it did in the dreams."

"For the first time since that dream, I'm feeling a heavy sense of dread," Ginny said to Brad as she watched the Smith's walk to their car.

"I know," Brad said. "Let's go home, regroup and decide what we're going to do with the little amount of time we have left. Garrett said he and Mark would make a last delivery no later than three this afternoon."

Ginny and Brad decided to go into Elkin and eat an early lunch at their favorite hamburger restaurant. Afterwards, they made one final trip to the large discount store. They added essentials they knew they could always use to their cart.

Ginny passed by the children's section. She paused, then picked up diapers, baby blankets, baby clothes, toddler clothes, formula, bottles and baby food. Moving on, Ginny added more children's clothes, socks, underwear and shoes in various sizes. She even filled a second cart with the same type of items. Brad watched her, surprised.

On the way home, Brad decided to ask Ginny about the purchases.

"Ginny, I have to ask, why the baby and children's items?"

Ginny hesitated, searching for the right words.

"I hadn't thought about those things until they were right in front of me," she said. "Mike's wife is of childbearing age. Or some refugees fleeing the cities may come by, desperate to feed their baby."

Brad nodded in understanding but thought she was holding something back.

"Could it be you were thinking about yourself and what you may need?" he asked. Ginny didn't answer. "Ginny, in my dream you and Pete fell in love. Do you think that's a real possibility if this does happen as we saw?"

Ginny took a deep breath and leaned back against the passenger seat headrest, staring straight ahead.

"I don't know. It was a dream. I felt very real emotions in it, but how do I know if that's what will happen? I think it's wise to get these things regardless of what will happen with my life. Who knows, Brad, you may meet a girl passing through and need those things for yourself."

"I kind of hope so, Ginny," he said. "And I hope the same for you. It will be a hard time, and it would be nice to have a partner to lean on."

"Thanks for understanding," Ginny said, nodding in agreement. "If there's time after Mark and Garrett leave, I may come back for more baby products, especially diaper rash creams, baby shampoo, baby medications. You know what I mean."

"I do," Brad said, "and I'll come with you. We can fill up two carts." Ginny smiled.

That afternoon, Garrett, Mark, Ginny and Brad sat around the dining room table reviewing everything they had done. It was amazing what they had accomplished in five days while still juggling their jobs.

"I don't know if we could do anything else," Mark said. "We could house our families here for a year with what we have. The others are also bringing supplies, which will help. Can anyone think of anything else?"

Garrett cleared his throat.

"I thought of something," he said. "I've been thinking about a second career in ministry for a while now. I bought several commentaries and Bible studies that I have stored in our bedroom."

He pulled out a certificate from a file of papers and receipts.

"I know this isn't like going to seminary, but I contacted an online church that has the same theology as we're used to. I went through a crash course over three days, and today I received this in an email." Garrett showed them the certificate. "I'm ordained in the church listed below and registered with North Carolina as eligible to do weddings, funerals, baptisms, and services."

Everyone was speechless. Then Ginny broke the silence.

"That's wonderful Garrett. I had thought you would be our informal spiritual advisor during all this, but this is perfect."

"Congratulations, Garrett," Mark said, "but I'm not surprised. I've thought for a while now that you might be considering ministry."

"I think it's great, Garrett" Brad said. "You will be our strength and our reminder not to depend solely on ourselves."

"Well," Mark said, shifting in his seat. "I think we've done all that we can do. I have an hour's drive home, and I'm tired. I think I need to get on the road."

"I agree," Garrett said, "but let's end this with prayer."

The four held hands while Garrett asked God for his blessings, strength, protection, and forgiveness.

"Well, I guess this is it," Garrett said. "Tomorrow at this time, we will know if we have been prudent or reckless. Personally, I hope we can joke about this and consider ourselves reckless." The others agreed.

Brad watched Mark's and Garrett's vehicles disappear down the drive. He turned to Ginny.

"Let's go back to the store. We have time to get a few carts full of items for babies and small children. What about childbirth supplies? Can you get those there?"

"We can improvise," Ginny said. "I think those bulb syringes used to clean out ears will work. Good scissors, mild soap, betadine. I think we can find those."

"Let's go," Brad said. "We can plan on the way."

At the store, Brad and Ginny filled three carts with supplies. They bought every pack of cloth diapers they could find along with mild clothes detergent formulated for babies. Ginny grinned at Brad when she threw in breast feeding pumps and supplies.

"I don't even want to think about that," he said, making Ginny laugh.

A last pass down the coffee section, candy aisle and the dairy and meat counters filled another cart. They left the store just as it was closing.

"I'm glad we did this," Ginny said on the ride back to the farm. "I feel good about it, and I would have been a nervous wreck at home."

"Yeah," Brad said, "I'm nervous about tomorrow, too. Imagine the look on the faces of the people who run the shelters when we unload all this baby stuff because our dreams turn out to be just that, dreams."

"I hope that happens, Brad," Ginny said, sounding wishful.

CHAPTER 8

APRIL 10

North Carolina, USA

Ginny's alarm sounded at six am, but she was already up and dressed. Anxiety had made sleep elusive during the night. She looked at herself in the mirror. She looked just as she had when she'd left for the airport in her dream. Same clothes, same ponytail, same hat. Her carry-on bag was packed with the very same items she had packed in her dream.

During their preparations, Ginny gave a lot of thought to her supplements and the possible contract with the pet food company. She decided that she would still go to St. Louis if nothing happened. She was curious about what the Pure Pet Company wanted to offer her. But more than that, they had to know if Mark's friends were at the airport.

As Ginny poured herself a cup of coffee, she smiled as she thought of all the cases of coffee and carbonated beverages stacked in the basement. If she had to go through an apocalypse, she was going to have her coffee and bubbles.

"You need to eat, Ginny," Brad said as he came into the kitchen.

"It's highly possible that you may not get the chance for several hours."

"I have protein bars in my bag and a bottle of water for the truck," she said. "I'll get a couple bottles of water when I get through security. I'm just so nervous. The rest of my life will be decided this morning. Either we were right, or we weren't. Both will have consequences." She looked at the clock. "I guess it's time."

She took her bag to the truck, waved to Brad and drove down the driveway. An hour later, she had parked and was heading into the main terminal. Walking toward the security entrance, Ginny heard a voice behind her.

"Ginny Reed?"

Ginny turned and smiled when she saw the tall man with light brown skin and amber eyes.

"Alex Freeman?" she asked.

"That would be me," he answered.

"If you know me, then you must have had a dream, too," she said, tilting her head and taking in his appearance. She noted the airport security guard uniform.

"Yes," he said. "Pete called me. It turned out that he and I had the same dream, but we felt that we weren't supposed to contact Mark or your family."

"That's how Mark felt about you two," she said. "He said it was like we were supposed to be the proof to each other that we had been warned." Ginny looked around. "Is Pete in Greensboro? You said you talked with him."

"He's at my home," Alex said. "I came out to the terminal lobby to get you."

"Don't you have to work?" she asked. "What if we're wrong and you jeopardize your job?"

"I changed shifts," Alex said, giving Ginny a huge grin. "I'm just getting off mine. There are enough personnel to shut down the airport without my help. We can leave anytime."

Their conversation was interrupted when the televisions in the lobby sounded an alarm and switched to the emergency alert system. The monitors blinked, and the flights leaving Greensboro were cancelled, just like in the dream. Ginny's heart dropped to her stomach with a sense of dread.

"I guess this is it," Ginny said with a shaky voice. She turned back to Alex. "It really was a vision."

"Come on," Alex said quietly. "Let's get out of here. I moved my SUV to the short term parking lot where I knew you would park your truck."

Ginny blinked. "The truck? You know about my truck?"

"Yep," Alex said, grinning. "Sweet ride, vintage F100."

Alex took Ginny's bag, and they hurried out of the main doors of the airport. They walked across the street to the short term parking lot. The two vehicles happened to be near each other, and Alex put the bag in Ginny's truck.

"You may still remember the way, but I'll lead just in case," Alex said, walking toward his SUV.

"Lead on," Ginny replied, nodding in agreement.

Thirty minutes later they were parking in front of Alex's apartment. Erica came out of the apartment and gave her a hug.

"I knew you'd come," she said.

"You had the dream too?" asked Ginny.

"Yes," Erica said. "I know we've never met, but I feel like I've known you for years."

"And me too," said another much deeper voice behind Erica.

Ginny looked around, and there was Pete. She was stunned.

"Don't I get a hug, too?" he asked, throwing his arms wide in invitation.

Ginny needed no encouragement, she launched herself into Pete's arms. She was shocked. In reality, she was just meeting him, but his arms felt familiar and secure. She fit into his embrace just like she remembered.

Pete hugged her tightly.

"I already know I love you," he whispered.

"I know," she murmured into his chest. "I love you too."

"I want to introduce you to some people who weren't in the dream," Pete said as he took her hand, gripping it as though he was afraid she would pull away.

Pete introduced her to Max Benton and Sharon Ingram, two friends who were his highly trained administrative employees.

"Nice to meet you," Ginny said as she shook their hands. "Welcome to the farm."

She looked at Pete. "Somehow I don't think we need to go buy you clothes and toiletries this time."

"No," Pete answered. "I packed up and drove down. Everything I have of value is in my SUV and an enclosed trailer. Max and Sharon have their own overpacked SUV and a motor home to share." He pointed to the back of the parking lot at a new, large RV shining in the sun.

Ginny looked at her friends whom she had met by way of a dream. "Let's go home," she said.

Everyone was packed and ready to go. They exchanged phone numbers and created a caravan with Ginny in the lead. They made better progress this time. Thanks to everyone's preparation, they made it west of Winston-Salem before the roads were congested.

A few minutes into the drive home, Ginny called Brad.

"Hey," he said. "What happened?"

"I'm on my way home with Pete, Alex, Erica, and a couple of Pete's friends," Ginny said, smiling despite her nerves. "I'm just letting you know that my truck plus three SUVs, a sedan, and a motor home are coming your way, all loaded to the brim with supplies."

"I was hoping we were wrong," Brad said sadly, "but I saw the emergency screens on the TV. Thanks for giving me a heads up about the vehicles. I'll make spaces for them to park. We may need to build another pole barn. I didn't think about that."

Ginny called Mark and Garrett to let them know she was coming back with Alex, Erica, Pete and Pete's friends. Mark, Garrett and the Dickson's had kept their children out of school. As soon as they saw the televisions switch to emergency broadcasting and heard from Ginny, they prepared to leave Winston and drive to the farm.

Before going to the farm's driveway, Ginny stopped at a local gas station and convenience store. She filled her tank and waited while the others did the same. When she went inside to pay for her gas, the owner was watching them through the window.

"Good morning, Hal," Ginny said.

"Are all these people with you?" Hal asked, looking at Ginny then back out the window.

"Yes," Ginny answered. "They're coming to the farm to stay with us for a while."

"Doc," he said, sounding worried. "Do you know something I don't know and that maybe I need to know?"

"Hal," Ginny said, "I have a feeling that things are going to get very, very bad, and so do my brothers and their friends. May I suggest you make some calls and get as many deliveries as you can get today, especially gasoline. Take everything of value home with you, including food. Then lock your tanks. You may not do that today, but I suspect by tomorrow or the next day you'll be glad you did."

"I wondered what I should do when I heard about that nuclear missile that had been launched toward us," Hal said, gesturing to the television that hung in the corner of the store. "Even though it detonated over the ocean, I sent Hazel to the grocery store as soon as we saw the news. It didn't do any damage, but I was scared there may be more."

"That was smart, Hal," Ginny said. "Get everything you need now. Don't wait. If all this blows over, you can sit back and not fight the crowds for a week or so. And get your garden planted sooner than later."

"Thanks, Doc," Hal said. "I'm glad somebody else has the same anxiety over all this that I do." Hal paused. "Doc, will you still be making house calls?"

"For as long as I can, Hal," Ginny answered, giving him a reassuring smile. "If you need me, call me. You have some great beef and beautiful horses." She paused for a moment. "Get Bart out of school early today. Have him get a load of that good alfalfa hay from the Bradford's farm and some feed from the co-op in Elkin. That and grass should get you through the summer at least."

"Thanks, Doc," he said. "I'll lock the tanks after today, but if you need gas, you call me."

"Thanks, Hal." Ginny said as she left the store and returned to the pumps where the last of the vehicles had just been refueled. She looked at the group.

"The next stop is the farm," she said.

Everyone got back into their cars and trucks and followed Ginny.

Pete saw the sign for Lawson Farm Road as he followed Ginny. He remembered this from the dream. So far, he was amazed at how accurate those dreams had been.

Chapter 9

April 10

Brad watched the caravan of vehicles coming up the drive. Part of him was relieved they had gotten here safely, but he was mostly sad that the dreams had been this accurate. He went to each vehicle and told the driver where to park and followed them with his four-wheeler and trailer. Max parked the motor home next to the travel trailers.

Brad shook hands with Alex and Pete.

"I know that technically this is the first time I'm meeting you," Brad said, "but I feel like I have known you for a long time."

"I know what you mean," Alex said. "This is crazy. I tried telling some family members and close friends about the dream, but no one believed me."

Pete introduced Max and Sharon to Brad.

"They brought a motor home to live in," Pete said. "I hope you don't mind."

Brad looked at Max and Sharon.

"Welcome to the farm," he said. "I'm glad you're here."

"Thank you," Max said as he shook Brad's hand. "We appreciate your letting us stay. Sharon and I have seen on deployments what can happen when war comes or governments collapse. It'll get ugly, and I promise we will do everything we can to help keep this farm safe and productive."

"We appreciate that," Brad said.

Pete walked up to Ginny.

"I thought this place was beautiful in the dream, but this is beyond belief," he said, looking around.

"Thanks," she said. "We love it, and I know you will, too."

Ginny helped the group unload their vehicles. It took several trips with the trailer to get their possessions and supplies to the house and equipment shed. They were just about finished when Mark and Ceely, his wife, drove their truck and SUV up the drive.

Mark got out of the truck and hugged Ginny.

"How are you doing?" Mark asked her. "Was it weird at the airport when you met Alex and Pete?"

"They changed the dream," Ginny told him. "It's crazy, but we can have different outcomes." Ginny made her point when she introduced Mark to Max and Sharon who had followed Pete from Chicago.

Brad continued to unload luggage and supplies while everyone talked and got to know each other, or reacquainted, however you wanted to look at it. He still had trouble believing he knew all these people when, in reality, this was the first time he was meeting them.

The sound of arriving cars made Brad stop what he was doing. Garrett and the Dickson's were coming up the driveway. He breathed a sigh of relief. Almost everyone was here, and this time there was no anxiety about getting out of the cities. Again, Brad watched Garrett and Robert greet Pete and Alex like old friends. Barbara and Leah hugged Erica and Ceely and introduced themselves to Sharon.

"Hey, Uncle Brad."

Brad turned to see Adam and Brett, Garrett's twin sons, and Michael, the Dickson's son. The teenagers were only fourteen-years-old, but they conveyed the seriousness of the events taking place.

"Hey yourself," Brad replied. "How was the trip in?"

"Not like the last time," Adam said.

Brad looked at him questioningly.

"We had the dream too, Uncle Brad," Brett said.

Brad looked at them. "Well, I guess God sees you three as men capable of contributing to the wellbeing of the farm. Did you tell your parents?"

The boys nodded yes.

"Good," Brad said. "This isn't a time to keep secrets and worry about your place in this new life."

"Michael, did you have the dream, too?" Brad asked.

"Yes, Sir," Michael replied.

"We all had it," Adam said. "The three of us got together and made some plans of our own."

"Oh yeah?" Brad raised his eyebrows. "What did you do?"

Brett grinned. "I sold my drone and some other equipment then bought the best drone on the market. It will fly higher and farther than what I used to have. I also bought other electronic devices and software for tracking drones."

Adam went to the SUV and came back carrying a kennel.

"I adopted a dog and started training it to be a guard dog," he said. "He's smart. I also bought some high-tech game cameras for surveillance."

Brad picked up the young dog and examined him closely. He noticed their dog, Barf, wagging his tail and trying to sniff the puppy.

"You made a great choice, Adam," Brad said. "This is a good breed for training for protection. Michael, what did you do?"

"I bought heritage seeds of a bunch of vegetables, herbs and flowers, and I brought young fruit trees and bushes," Michael told him.

"Yeah?" Brad asked, smiling. "What kind of trees?

"Apple, cherry, pear, and peach trees," Michael said. "Also, blueberry, blackberry, and raspberry bushes."

"You guys are the best," Brad said. "I guess this time we include you in all the adult discussions."

Max walked over and looked at the dog.

"Who's pup?" he asked.

"Mine," Adam replied.

"I'm Max," he said, extending his hand. "Sharon and I came with Pete. I used to work with this breed in the Army. Do you plan to train him?"

"Yes, Sir," Adam said, shaking Max's hand. "His name is Brute. He's already learned basic commands like come and sit, and he's house broken. But I've only had him a couple days."

"That's impressive for just a couple days," Max said, scratching the puppy's ears. "Brute's a smart fellow. I can help you train him if you like."

"That would be great," Adam said enthusiastically.

"When we get settled, you can show me what he can do," Max said, reaching down to give Barf equal attention. "Then we'll discuss what you want him to learn.

Brad felt his stomach growl and was glad when Ginny called out from the back porch that lunch was ready. The boys shouted with relief and started to run toward the house. They stopped when they heard Mark's shrill whistle. Everyone quieted and waited for Mark to speak.

"Before we descend upon the kitchen," Mark said, holding out his hands and gesturing for their new friends and family members to gather closer. "We should take a moment to thank God for our safe arrival and the food we are about to eat." He looked at Garrett. "You got this."

Garrett gave a blessing of thanks then turned to Ginny. "Any instructions, Ginny?"

"Everyone has a red plastic cup with his or her name on it," Ginny said. "Keep that cup. They will be washed and reused until they fall apart. Other than that, everything is self-explanatory." She looked at the boys. "Okay, go eat."

The adults followed the younger kids into the house. Brad stayed in the back of the group and was the last to enter the kitchen. He knew these people, but after the stress of getting everything ready on the farm and still remembering Holly's rejection, he just didn't feel like socializing. He smiled when he saw the extra picnic tables he bought were being used by the kids and even some adults. That had been a good purchase.

Brad made a sandwich, found the cup with his name on it and filled it with tea. He took an empty seat at the table and started to eat. Listening to the conversations around him, he was intrigued by what he already knew about those who had been with them in the dream, but he was very interested in hearing Max and Sharon telling the others about themselves. They were regional managers for Pete's security company and were planning to help him manage his responsibilities and staff during the crisis.

When everyone had finished eating, Mark called the adults together for a meeting. He included Adam, Brett, and Michael, but the younger kids went outside to play in the yard.

"Well," Mark said, "here we are. I don't know what the future will bring, but I am so relieved that we will be together. This is a crazy question, but were your dreams detailed enough to remember how the work and responsibilities were divided?"

"I was assigned to meals, menus and medical duty," Ceely said. "But as I recall, we all pitched in everywhere as needed."

Barbara said, "I had inventory logistics and meals."

Robert said, "I had the garden, outhouse, and outdoor shower. Michael brought fruit trees and bushes." He looked at Brad and Ginny. "If you'll tell us where you want them, we'll get them in the ground this afternoon."

Pete said, "Mark, Alex and I had security, but I would like to add Max, Sharon and Bennett to that."

"Done," Mark said.

Ginny raised her hand. "I had medical supplies and community health with Ceely and Erica. I would like to add Sharon to that since she's a medic. My friend Jacque is coming, but she's still traveling from High Point. I'm hoping she gets here today. She's a physician and will probably lead our medical team."

"Done," Mark replied.

"I have the farm with Mark, Garrett, and Ginny," Brad said.

Adam shyly raised his hand, trying to be a supportive member of the group.

"Brett, Michael and I are in charge of lawn care and are to help wherever we're needed."

"This is unbelievable," Mark said, looking around the crowded dining room table and smiling. "We all had the same dreams and remember so much. Mike has agreed to work on any construction needs. Robert, he can help you with the outhouse and outdoor shower. Heather said she will start school lessons." He paused. "We've all been extremely busy. Has anyone checked the internet for updates in the news?"

Brett stood. "Adam, Michael and I have been monitoring different news feeds. The president addressed the nation and talked about the North Koreans launching nuclear missiles. Even though they detonated over the ocean and caused no damage to us, the president declared a national state of emergency.

"The mayors of all the big cities have issued curfews. Food shortages are already taking place and the roads are congested, mostly with people trying to get home from wherever they were when everything started this morning. All flights are cancelled in both the United States and Canada. Canada has also declared a state of emergency."

The group was quiet.

"Well," Mark said, "so far, the dreams have been extremely accurate. For now, I guess we finish unloading and settle in before we start working in our assigned task groups. Does anyone have anything else?"

Ginny raised her hand. "I haven't made room assignments, but I'm guessing you already know where you're bunking."

The adults laughed.

"Already unloaded our belongings into the room," Ceely said.

"Us too," replied Erica and Leah.

"The bed is made and the remote nearby," Pete said grinning.

"Glad I asked!" Ginny said with a light chuckle. "I did decide to move the girls into the spare room upstairs in the old section. I remembered from the dream how scared they were in the basement when the power went out. Also, I still need to clear out the clinic. I didn't do that ahead of time because I kept it open until Saturday." She looked at Pete and Mark. "Can you guys help me with that again?"

"Sure," Mark said. "When do you want to do that?"

"Let's go this afternoon," Ginny said. "It's closed. Everyone will be glued to the TV, and we won't have to worry about lights shining in the dark like we did in the dream."

"Okay," Mark said. "Pete, Alex, Max, and I will go with you as soon as we're done here."

"We'll need an extra truck this time," Ginny said. "I ordered a lot of supplies."

"Anyone have anything else?" Mark asked. No one answered. "All right then. Everyone back to whatever you were doing, and we'll get the supplies from the clinic."

Brad went back to the four-wheeler and helped people unload the rest of their belongings. He watched Ginny and the other men leave to go to the clinic to get Ginny's medical supplies. He hoped the relationship between Ginny and Pete was real and not just a figment of the dream. She deserved a husband and family, and he hoped Pete would be the one.

When everything had been unloaded, Brad approached Michael.

"Let me see your trees," he said.

Michael took him to the shady side of the equipment shed where the trees and bushes were leaning against the wall. Brad looked at the labels and studied each plant.

"These look good, Michael," Brad said. "You bought quality stock."

Michael beamed with pride at Brad's praise.

Brad turned his attention to the driveway when he heard a car coming to the house. Mark's brother-in-law, Mike, and his family had arrived. Brad was relieved. They were all here now, like they were in the dream. Brad showed them where to park then led them to the campers where they would be living.

Just before dinner, while everyone was standing around the kitchen and den, cell phones began sounding with emergency notifications. The noise cut through the chatter like a blade. Everyone froze.

The terrorists had detonated conventional and dirty bombs in several cities and at the Pentagon. Those were the attacks in the dreams, but in the visions, they had happened the next morning. This was different. More cities had been hit than had been in their dream, and the timeline had shifted by nearly twelve hours.

A heavy silence settled over the house. Knowing the dreams could be changed for the better had given them a sense of calm, but this change was worse. It was a rude awakening. They had almost become complacent, and this reminded them that they could not let their guard down.

While the children stayed inside, the adults discreetly watched the coverage on their phones as they moved through their tasks. The kitchen was cleaned. Mark, Pete, Alex, Bennett, and Max separated the game cameras and planned where they would be placed the next day. Some of the adults gathered in the back yard to watch the teenagers play corn hole, trying to maintain a sense of normalcy. Ginny slipped onto the front porch and sat in the swing, where Pete joined her.

Brad watched the activity around him. The day had been nothing but organized chaos, but it had worked. Then the cities were bombed today, and reality hit like a slap. His thoughts drifted to Holly, and the sting of her rejection washed over him again. Suddenly, he felt he had to get out of the house and away from people.

He headed for the front door but stopped when he heard Pete and Ginny talking on the porch. He hadn't meant to listen, but their voices carried. They were discussing their dreams. He was glad when he heard Pete say he didn't know if he had been shot. Brad thought no one needed an ending to that scene in the dream. It could be changed. They all knew that now. He just wondered if anyone realized Holly was absent. Everyone had gotten here earlier than they had in the dream, but Holly had not come at all.

He felt trapped. He couldn't go out the front door, and he didn't want to go out the back and risk people asking where he was going. He just wanted to find a place where there were no people. He didn't want anyone to ask about Holly; he didn't want to face the pity and compassion he would see in their eyes when he explained that she wouldn't be coming. He felt disconnected and adrift from his own life.

Brad sighed, turned and walked to the office. He closed the door and laid down on the futon. After starting a movie on his electronic pad, he put the headphones on and tuned out the world.

CHAPTER 10

APRIL 11

In the large chalet just outside Davos, The Committee, which consisted of five of the richest men in Europe and the United States, sat in a spacious dining room eating an early breakfast. With them were representatives from various countries across the world.

They listened as the representative of the Chinese Government gave his report. North Korea had launched and successfully detonated a nuclear EMP over the Pacific Ocean. The U.S. Government had been completely surprised, and the President had declared a national state of emergency. All air travel had been suspended in both Canada and the United States.

John Rosen, the leader of The Committee, raised a glass of orange juice, "Gentlemen, to the success of phase one."

He looked at the aide to the U.S. National Security Advisor, Jacob Miller.

"Mr. Becker," he said, "How are things in the United States?" John already knew the answer to his question, but he wanted the young American to voice his government's perspective.

Greg Becker gave Rosen a smile bordering on arrogance.

"The state of emergency has ushered in martial law, which has caused widespread panic," Greg said. "Citizens are fighting each other for supplies and gasoline. Police officers are struggling to maintain peace in the chaos. Mr. Miller is cautioning the President and his advisors to not retaliate against North Korea because no damage was done to the U.S."

John nodded in approval. He looked at his watch then back at Greg.

"Phase two should have started about twelve hours ago. Does Mr. Miller have a report on that?"

"The terrorists detonated bombs in twenty-five different cities as well as at the Pentagon," Greg said. "Areas of the electrical grid, selected harbors, and crucial manufacturing plants for drugs, steel, and food were also targeted. Major interstate highway bridges across the Mississippi, Colorado, Ohio, and Missouri rivers have been confirmed as destroyed or compromised enough to halt traffic. Most were conventional bombs with C4, but dirty bombs with radioactive material were detonated in Chicago, Los Angeles, New York, Seattle, Atlanta, and Boston. Search and rescue efforts continued through the night, but the destruction is extensive, as was planned."

Greg Becker's phone vibrated in his pocket. He excused himself and answered with a crisp, "Yes, Sir," then listened. After a few minutes, he ended the call and returned to the room.

John finished his remarks then turned to Greg.

"Mr. Becker, I assume you just heard from Mr. Miller?"

"Yes, Sir," Greg said. "Mr. Miller said to let you know that the U.S. Government is in a state of chaos and confusion. They were not expecting the terrorist attacks. Various terrorist groups from multiple countries are taking credit for the attacks, so no one has any idea who to blame."

"Well done," Rosen said. "Congratulations, everyone. Phase three is also underway." He looked at the stock market app on his phone.

"We managed to sell a lot of stocks Friday afternoon. We sold more in the futures markets and were able to sell even more as soon as the markets opened in New York yesterday." John looked at the representatives from China, Russia, India, South Africa and Brazil. "Gentlemen, were your countries able to dump the U.S. Treasuries like we wanted?"

Mr. Lin from China looked up from his computer long enough to answer.

"Yes," he said. "All of our countries were successful. We started releasing small amounts of treasuries last week. The rest were released during yesterday's Asian and European markets. We managed to get rid of some more as soon as trading opened in the U.S. yesterday. We have very few American Treasury Bonds left."

John Rosen smiled and raised his glass of orange juice again.

"Here's to a successful beginning of the downfall of the United States and the new world order that will rise from the ashes."

The representative from the Chinese government looked troubled.

"Your report sounds promising for an early start to this venture," he said. "However, I thought we agreed to limit or omit dirty bombs. Did the bombs with radioactive material avoid the natural resources as China requested?"

"They were supposed to," John answered. "No one wants to ruin the natural resources of the richest country in the world. American land is valuable. According to our reports, the farmland is secure, and the waters are not polluted."

The Chinese representative nodded and turned back to his laptop, apparently pleased with the Rosen's answer.

With the business concluded, the room settled into low conversation and the gentle clink of silverware on fine china as the group resumed their breakfast.

Washington, DC

Jacob Miller, the National Security Advisor to President Massey, yawned. The early morning sun filtered through the windows of his office, catching the small column of steam rising from his cup of government-issued coffee. He should have been exhausted, but he wasn't. He felt energized. Yesterday was successful, and the country was in a disorganized panic. He had made a lot of money selling his financial investments the week before and shifting the money into real estate in Canada, Belize, and the Bahamas. Now, another big bonus from The Committee was on its way.

What pleased Jacob even more was how completely blindsided President Massey had been and how dependent he was on Jacob's advice. The man had no idea what to do next. Jacob had emphasized that there was no guarantee that North Korea's missiles were aimed at the United States and could have even been a nuclear test. He cautioned against retaliation.

Then there was phase two, which had been unexpected and even more successful. While everyone was fixated on the nuclear missiles, no one had been watching domestic targets when the terrorist bombs detonated. He smiled; more chaos was coming. Two successful surprises for the United States meant two substantial bonuses in his Swiss bank account. If only he could gain control of the Federal Reserve and the Stock Market, then his plan would be perfect.

Donald Evans, the Secretary of Defense, rubbed his tired eyes. He had gotten barely three hours of sleep since North Korea launched that nuclear weapon. It had detonated just before reaching the apex of its assent, which meant they could not get a precise target from its downward trajectory. The Military was sure it was heading somewhere along the west coast of the United States, which was highly populated. The death toll of a nuclear attack in any part of that area would have been unthinkable. As that update came through, the surprise terrorist attacks plunged the nation into a deeper sense of fear and panic.

Unfortunately, the National Security Advisor, Jacob Miller, kept advising the president to not retaliate. His advice had merit, but something about his behavior felt off to Donald. They had worked together for the two years, and Miller had been a serious, dedicated member of the Cabinet. Now, he almost seemed pleased. It was as if he could barely contain a smile. Donald shook his head. Everyone was on edge. Everyone was anxious. The slightest deviation in behavior could be misread. He would have to remember that.

CHAPTER 11

APRIL 11

North Carolina, USA

Brad woke up early again. He hadn't slept well and already felt tired. He laid in bed for a moment, thinking about all he needed to do. It was complicated. Mark was planning projects for everyone to work on, but he still needed to do the farm work. Also, everyone looked to him and Ginny as hosts, constantly asking questions. It was a lot to handle, and it could be a struggle to stay in a good mood and not become grumpy. They didn't need that yet. Eventually, tensions would flare, but he didn't want it to be on the second day because of his lack of sleep.

Dressed and ready to work, Brad walked into the kitchen. Ginny and Pete were sitting at the island talking. He went to the cabinet and poured himself a cup of coffee. Taking his coffee back to the office, Brad made a list of supplies to get at the lumber yard. He wanted to build a pole barn on his new property. They could park some of the vehicles there, but he'd rather use the space to store the hay from Ginny's land and let everyone keep their cars and trucks nearby. Thinking about hay, Brad realized he needed to fertilize the pastures and hay strips on his new farm.

Garrett poked his head into the office.

"Good morning," he said. "Everyone is eating breakfast. I thought I would let you know."

"Thanks. I'll be right there," Brad said. He looked at Garrett and gave him the ghost of a smile. "I was just making a list of supplies I need to go get from the lumber yard this morning before everything is gone. I want to build a pole barn on the Thompson property that I now own."

"You own that?" Garrett asked. "That's great. Congratulations."

"Thanks," Brad said with a grin. "I'm pretty happy about it, and I'm glad it was settled before yesterday. Now I don't have to worry about anyone snapping it up before all this catastrophe mess settles down."

Brad stood and walked with Garrett into the kitchen.

"Need some company on your errand?" Garrett asked. "I'll be glad to go with you."

"Thanks. That would be helpful."

Brad had just made a plate of eggs, bacon and toast when news alerts sounded on cell phones.

Pete turned to Garrett. "I seem to recall it was Brett who gave us an update on the things that happened last night."

Brett, Adam, and Michael ran up the stairs from the basement and into the kitchen. They held up their phones.

"We have the latest news," Brett said.

The dining room quieted as everyone set down their forks to listen to the updates.

"Reports have come in about the terrorist attacks with both conventional bombs and dirty bombs," Brett said, not taking his eyes off his phone screen as he spoke. "Some of the places hit include Chicago, New York City, San Diego, San Francisco, Portland, Miami, Washington DC, Seattle, and Houston. Local news channels say that bombs went off in Charlotte, but we don't know the extent of the damage. Their TV stations are offline. This says there were smaller, more strategically placed bombs that went off, too. The Pentagon was hit. Other targets included some bridges across major rivers, harbors, and various refineries and manufacturing plants."

"Just like the dream," Barbara said softly, "only worse."

Everyone looked at Pete.

"We knew this would happen," Pete said, looking around at the group. "Before I left, I told everyone I knew that if North Korea launched a missile, they needed to get out of the city immediately, because Chicago would be a big target."

"Did they listen?" Garrett asked.

"I don't know," Pete answered. "I left town right after I sounded the alarm. I hope they did."

Ginny's phone rang.

"This is Dr. Reed," she answered. She met Pete's eyes as she stepped into the hall to take the call. The rest of the group stayed silent; the only sound was Ginny's muffled voice until she ended the call and came back into the room.

"Well, that's the same call I got in the dream," she said. "I need to go next door. The Johnson's mare is about to foal."

"Okay. Be safe," Mark said. "We'll see you when you get back."

Ginny gathered her medical records and went to her truck. She was well prepared with supplies and would have no problem doing the work she needed to do.

After Brett announced the news, Brad stood and told Mark he was going to the lumber yard and that Garrett was going with him.

"Do you want someone else to go for added protection?" Mark asked.

"No," Brad said. "I have a shotgun in the truck, and I can get another one. Garrett's handy with firearms, so we should be okay.

Besides, the lumber yard isn't in town. It's on this side but outside the city limits. I figure most people will be hunting groceries, not lumber."

Garrett helped Brad hitch the largest trailer he owned to the back of the farm truck, and they left.

On the way to Elkin, Garrett said, "Brad, is everything all right? You seem quieter than usual. I noticed that Holly isn't here. Did something happen?"

"Yes," Brad answered with a heavy sigh. "As soon as you and Mark left that first evening, I went to see Holly. I told her about the dreams. I asked her to marry me that week and come to the farm to live. She told me no. She wanted a big wedding, not a hasty ceremony. Then she called me a crazy kook and said she had no intention of living through any kind of catastrophe with a bunch of Bible-thumping crazies."

"I'm sorry, Brad," Garrett said softly, reaching over and touching his brother's shoulder. "I know that hurt."

"It did at first," Brad replied. "Garrett, what I hate the most is that I lost my temper. I told her if nothing happened, she could call me a crazy kook. But if it happened like I thought it would, she had lost her chance. I told her not to come knocking on my door asking for my help. That was when she said there was no way she would ever do that because she didn't want to be trapped with a bunch of Bible thumpers. I couldn't believe how wrong I was about her. I just stood up and left. I haven't seen her since, and she hasn't tried to contact me."

Garrett was quiet for a moment.

"Brad," he said, "I do believe God is looking out for you. He showed you early that you and Holly would not have been happy together. I firmly believe that He will send you the perfect mate, even in an apocalypse. Look what He did for Ginny. She and Pete are great together. The hard part is working through your emotions about what you thought you had with Holly and then being patient for your own healing and whatever God sends your way."

"Yeah," Brad said, nodding. "That's hard. I know I haven't been very social since all of this started, but I just haven't wanted to be around people."

"That's understandable," Garrett said. "I'm guessing Ginny knows what happened?"

"Yes," Brad answered. "She noticed things were different with me the other day. We talked, and she agrees with what you just said. In fact, her words were almost identical to yours."

"That's the way with siblings sometimes." Garrett paused. "Brad, we don't have to make a blanket announcement that Holly's not coming. If anyone asks, just say she chose to stay in Elkin, and that part of the dream is different."

"Thanks, Garrett," Brad said. "That sounds like a good plan. I know I dodged a bullet when she turned me down, but I had emotions tied up in the relationship that I guess she didn't. I'm still working through them, but I'll be fine. It's just going to take some time."

"Yes, you'll be fine," Garrett said. "In the meantime, I'm here if you want to vent. I can even run interference with the others if you don't want to talk about it."

"Thanks," Brad said, "but I can explain."

Brad turned into the lumber yard, and the conversation changed to the task at hand.

Ginny returned from the Johnson farm and parked behind the equipment shed. Mark was outside helping Robert mark off the area for the outhouse.

"That was fast," he said as he walked over to her truck.

"The mare was almost ready when I got there," Ginny said, turning toward him. "An easy delivery. A little filly."

"Garrett and Brad went to the lumber yard," Mark said, handing a measuring tape to Robert. "Brad wanted to get supplies to build a pole barn on the Thompson farm before poles, lumber and roofing ran out. Ginny, is Brad okay? I noticed he didn't go get Holly this morning."

Ginny shook her head and reached into the truck for her dirty supplies.

"Brad asked Holly to marry him and come live here," she said. "He told her about our dreams and what was going to happen. She called him a kook and broke up with him. He's hurting right now, and he doesn't want to answer questions, even those from well-meaning people."

Mark grimaced a sad face. "Ouch. That had to hurt. I won't ask him anything. I'll see if I can keep him busy."

"That won't be a problem," Ginny said. "This is spring. Busy time on the farm."

Mark nodded in agreement.

Ginny placed her soiled products in a large garbage barrel then walked back into the house. She stopped at the laundry room where she showered and changed before going into the kitchen.

"That was fast," Ceely said from the sink where she was washing dishes. "How's the horse?"

"Good," Ginny answered. "A little filly. The owner, Aaron, is going to pay me in fresh milk, butter, and cheese."

"That's wonderful!" Ceely exclaimed. "I talked with a friend in Winston. The stores are already out of dairy products and bread."

Ginny turned to Mark, who had walked into the kitchen.

"Aaron didn't have any type of forewarning. He said that he and Donna went into Elkin yesterday to get some supplies after they heard the news about the missiles."

"Interesting," Mark said. "I wonder if anyone else had a warning or if we're in the minority."

"Hal at the gas station said he had a sense that something bad was about to happen but couldn't put his finger on it," Ginny said. "Bob Smith had a detailed dream and has been preparing like we have. They're the only ones outside our group I've talked to who had any inkling that we might be on the edge of a catastrophe."

Ceely came over, kissed her husband on the cheek then turned to Ginny.

"Need a snack?" she asked.

"No, I just want to sit for a while and drink the bubbles," Ginny said, pulling a soda from the refrigerator and walking to the couch in the den.

Brad and Garrett pulled up next to the barn with a trailer full of lumber. Brad walked across the yard to where Robert and Mike were working and asked if they would help build the pole barn after the outhouse and outdoor shower were finished. They agreed, and Brad and Garrett headed off to park the trailer in the barn on Brad's property.

Several of the men spent the morning placing game cameras along the edges of the property. Alex and Bennett took the east and south sides of the farm along Lawson Farm Road. Pete and Max placed them on the north and west sides around the clinic and Brad's new house. Since the Thompsons had left for their son's residence the day before, the house now stood empty, and they would help Brad secure it.

The four returned to the house for lunch. When they went inside, Pete saw Ginny sitting on the couch with a soda in her hand. He walked over and sat beside her.

"How did it go?" he asked.

"Easy delivery," Ginny said. "Aaron asked if you would stop by and check his house for security. He didn't have any kind of dream or premonition, so they aren't prepared. This is taking them by surprise."

"We'll have the cameras up and running by this evening," Pete said. "Tell him we'll be over tomorrow."

Mark joined them in the den.

Ginny looked at the two men. "In my dream we spent this afternoon and tomorrow looking for supplies. Can you guys think of anything else we may need, or should we let it go?"

"In my opinion, we should stay here," Mark said. "We are more than well prepared. To go out again could put us in jeopardy. In my dream, I remember being concerned about people following us. If we stay, we eliminate that danger. Also, we get more done around here."

"Sounds good to me," Ginny said. "I remember being surprised by the anxiety that people in town had."

Lunch was leisurely. The adults sat around the table after eating, still getting to know each other. Finally, Pete and Max stood.

We need to go," he said. "We'll finish placing the cameras by later this afternoon. We should be able to monitor them on the computers starting tonight, even though I don't think we will need to for at least another 24 hours." Giving Ginny a smiling glance, Pete left through the back door.

"So," Mark said, leaning back in his chair. "I'm being nosy, but are you and Pete an item in real life like in the dream?"

"I think so," Ginny said. "We're taking it slow and not rushing things. Technically, we just met for the first time yesterday, even if we do feel like we've known each other longer."

"That's wise," Mark said. "I won't pry. I was just playing the role of big brother."

"No worries," Ginny said with a smile. "I like that you do."

CHAPTER 12

APRIL 11

North Carolina, USA

After dinner, Mark called the adults to a group meeting around the dining room table. Ginny got a legal pad to jot down notes, and he took updates from the others on their projects around the farm. The cameras were in place and their programs would be downloaded onto the computer after supper. The fruit trees and bushes were planted and the foundations for the outhouse and outdoor shower had been marked off with building to start the next day.

"The television has been off," Mark said and looked at Adam. "Have you guys been checking the internet for news?"

"I have the latest news," Adam said, sliding his chair back and standing. "Russia has increased their offensive and moved further into Ukraine. China has taken the opportunity to expand into the South China Sea and into islands Japan claims as theirs." He paused. "You know, it's like those two countries were just poised and waiting for this."

He continued, "North Korea is silent but so is the United States. It's almost like a game of chicken. Some commentators think there is a plan, but that the U.S. is drawing it out to make the dictator nervous. Others are very critical of the President because we haven't retaliated for the terrorist attacks. They're calling him weak and indecisive. NATO is condemning everybody and doing nothing. Europe is nervous and watching everything closely. It seems the only countries not currently affected are Australia, Iceland, and those in South America.

"The fallout from the dirty bombs is minimal because the radioactive material was not projected very far into the atmosphere, but it's making rescue and recovery difficult. Washington DC is on lockdown, and the area around the Pentagon is blocked. No one will be allowed to go into the city. Anyone can leave, but if you do, you can't return."

"One last item of interest," Adam said, "the terrorist attacks caused a lot of power outages. To get the cities back on track, power from other areas may be diverted. The report said to be prepared for rolling blackouts for the foreseeable future. I believe I gave this very same monologue in my dream."

Ginny's phone rang. Her eyes met Pete's across the table.

"This is Dr. Reed." She listened for a moment and said, "Yes. You're right. I'll be right there."

"Tom Sutton," Ginny said to the group after she ended the call. "He has a cow that delivered a calf then had a prolapsed uterus. It's crazy how this is just like the dream."

"Then I guess I'm going with you," Pete said, standing. "That's what I did in my dream."

"Well, he's just next door, and we both know we had no trouble," Ginny said. "You can stay here if you like."

"No," Pete said, pushing his chair back to the table. "The dreams have proven things can be changed. I won't take any chances on assuming things will be fine."

"Okay," Ginny said, standing. "Put on some old clothes and boots. I have a cow uterus to put back in place." The group groaned.

"I didn't need to know that," Heather said.

"Aunt Ginny, can I come too?" Adam asked.

Ginny looked at Garrett who nodded yes.

"Sure," she said. "Go put on old clothes. You can assist."

"Yes!" Adam exclaimed while pumping his fist. "I'll be right back."

Garrett watched Adam disappear down the stairs to the basement then looked back at Ginny.

"Thank you. Adam's been planning to go to NC State and then to vet school. Hopefully all this will be over by the time they're supposed to be graduating high school."

"I thought so," Ginny said. "He was a good assistant in the clinic last Christmas."

Adam came running back up the stairs. "I'm ready."

"Okay, come with me," Ginny said. "You can pull up my notes on the Sutton Farm on my tablet. It's sync'd with the clinic records."

Adam followed Ginny into the office. When they came out, Pete was waiting for them in the mudroom. They went outside and got into Ginny's work truck.

Tom Sutton met Ginny at his barn and told her to follow him. Wiry-built and just under six feet, he wore his usual wide-brimmed straw hat. Tom swung onto a four-wheeler and led her to a pasture that bordered a creek. His son, Brady, stood by a cow secured in a cattle chute. The scene was so similar to her dream that Ginny felt a jolt of amazement as she parked and got out of the truck.

Ginny shook Tom's hand. "Hello, Tom." She gestured to Pete and Adam, "This is Pete. He's a friend of Mark's and will be staying with us for a while. He's from Chicago."

"Nice to meet you," Tom said as he shook Pete's hand. "I'm sorry about Chicago. I'm glad you weren't there last night."

"Thank you, Tom," Pete said, "I'm glad, too. I came with Ginny to help, although I probably won't be able to do any more than hold a flashlight."

"Tom, this is my nephew, Adam," Ginny said, gesturing behind her where Adam held her supplies. "He wants to be a veterinarian, so he came to assist."

"Nice to meet you, Adam," Tom said. "That's my son, Brady, standing by the cow. You two look to be about the same age."

Adam said hello to both Tom and Brady.

Ginny opened the back of the trailer while the men set up the lights. She pulled on a protective gown, gloves and shoe covers before examining the cow. As she worked, she explained each step to Adam then told him to jump back when the cow was about to urinate. Ginny laughed at his reaction, finished cleaning the cow and put a small suture in place to prevent the uterus from prolapsing again.

When Pete helped her repack her equipment in the truck, Adam took the chance to talk with Brady. They were the same age, supposed to be finishing their freshmen year of high school. Ginny looked over at the teens. Even in the dark she could see their differences. Adam was slightly taller than Brady, and his blond hair contrasted to Brady's dark hair. She heard Adam tell Brady about his twin brother and a friend at the Reed farm, then invited him to come over and hang out whenever he had free time.

Tom had been watching and listening to the boys. He looked at Ginny.

"Your nephew is a nice young man," he said. "I appreciate him inviting Brady over. With schools being closed, it'll be hard on teenagers to not be with their friends."

"Adam, Brett, and Michael are good kids," Ginny replied. "Brady is welcome to come over any time. I think he'll fit in well with them." Tom thanked her.

Ginny was walking back to the truck when she caught sight of some cows lying down at the edge of the pasture. Her mind flashed to her memories of the dream. She turned and walked back to Tom.

"Tom, do you have any game cameras?"

"Yes," Tom answered. "Do you need some?"

"No," Ginny said. "I just thought you might want to put some around so you can keep tabs on your farm and cattle during all this. Hungry people could try taking small steers or calves for food."

"I know," Tom said. "Interesting you should say that. I put all I had around the farm yesterday. I can see my cows in the pasture and the road all the way to your drive. I can't tell you why I did it, but I just had the feeling I needed to. I even went into Elkin and bought extra cameras yesterday. Brady and I worked all day getting them up. They work well with the program we downloaded to live stream the pictures into the house. Brady's real good at that sort of thing."

"Good thinking, Tom," Ginny said, nodding in agreement. "What about your other son? Has he gotten back from Charlotte?"

"Not yet," Tom said, frowning. "He called yesterday and said he was on his way. He was driving but never arrived. I'm guessing he got caught in all the traffic they were showing on the news. I'm hoping the problem is he ran out of gas and is trying to get here on foot. Brady has a find my phone app and said he saw Jerry's phone near Elkin and moving slowly this way. At least it's on the move and not in one place. That would really worry me."

"Jerry's resourceful," Ginny said. "I'm sure he'll get here safe and sound." Ginny turned to walk back to her truck. "Call if you need anything. I'm going to get some sleep." Ginny walked back to her truck where Pete and Adam were waiting.

"Night, Doc," Tom said as he watched her walk away.

Ginny put a plastic sheet over the passenger seat then threw the keys to Pete. "You drive. I can't wait to get out of these clothes."

Adam climbed into the backseat, and the three drove back to the farm where Pete parked by the equipment shed.

"I'll take care of the trailer in the morning," Ginny said. She took the wad of soiled gloves and gown into the house and threw them in the trash.

Brad, who was still up, hurried by her, careful to keep several feet between them. He went into the office, slamming the door closed behind him.

"Nope, not getting near you," he said through the door.

Ginny started laughing. Adam looked at them in confusion.

"Adam," Ginny said, getting his attention. "Thank you for helping." With no warning, she gave him a big hug.

"Eww, Aunt Ginny!" he exclaimed, flinching away from her and wiping at his t-shirt. "That's gross! Now I have to shower!"

Ginny laughed harder.

Brad opened the door to the office and said loudly, "Run Adam. She loves getting cow piss on anyone nearby."

Ginny fell against the wall laughing. She looked around; Pete was nowhere to be seen. The door to his room cracked open, and his head peeked out, his eyes finding hers.

"I learned that lesson in the dream," Pete said, laughing.

Still laughing, Ginny straightened and stepped into the laundry room. She pulled the door closed, stripped out of her clothes and dropped everything straight into the washing machine before walking into the bathroom. A quick shower later, she slipped into the shorts and t-shirt she kept in there for post-call cleanups.

When she came back out, Pete was waiting at the kitchen island, a beer in one hand and a carbonated drink in the other. He handed her the soda.

"Want to sit on the porch or are you too tired?" he asked.

"Let's sit," Ginny said. "I always need to unwind after a late-night call."

They sat in the swing, talking, and watching the farm under the moonlight until Ginny yawned.

"Okay, now I need sleep," she said into her hand as she stood. "See you in the morning."

Pete stood. He hugged her and said, "Goodnight."

CHAPTER 13

APRIL 12

Two days after the first wave of attacks, President Douglas Massey sat in the Oval Office rubbing his tired, gritty eyes. Sipping an early-morning coffee, he sighed with frustration. He had been up all night in the Situation Room arguing with the Cabinet. More specifically, he had been arguing with Jacob Miller, the National Security Advisor.

Massey wanted to retaliate. They had traced residue from the terrorist bombs to Russia, China, Iran, Venezuela, South Africa and Brazil. He wanted to hit them, plus North Korea, all at once. Miller kept warning him off, reminding him there was no proof of who was actually responsible and no guarantee any of the bombs were state-sponsored. Massey lost his temper. Ignoring the consquences, Massey ordered a limited retaliation against North Korea. He could tell that Jacob Miller and Donald Evans, the Secretary of Defense, were not happy, but he didn't care. Public opinion was turning against him, and he wanted to show the world what happened when you messed with the United States. More than that, he wanted to show the world what happened when you messed with Douglas Massey. He wanted to be the hero.

To make matters worse, the Chairman of the Federal Reserve reported that countries around the world, especially China, had dumped their U.S. Treasury Bonds. Only the NATO countries still held U.S. Treasuries, and they were scrambling to unload them. The market was now flooded with no buyers except the Federal Reserve, and even they couldn't absorb the volume. An economic collapse was imminent if the situation didn't change. The Secretary of State was contacting every foreign diplomat in Washington, trying to discover the reasons behind the sudden sell-off.

Massey leaned back in his chair, stared at the ceiling, and thought about the problem with U.S. Treasuries. If they couldn't slow or stop the financial collapse coming their way, then he needed to figure out a way to turn it to his advantage, hopefully both politically and financially.

"Mr. President."

Massey turned to see his chief of staff, Abe Jenkins, approaching him.

"Yes?"

"Sir, the Secretary of State called," Jenkins said. "He said that most of the foreign diplomats stationed in Washington have left the country. Only NATO diplomats remain."

"What do you mean they've left the country?" Massey asked, sitting up straight and alert.

"According to the information he received," Jenkins continued, "their buildings are completely empty, with no staff, no paperwork. Empty. It's thought that this was completed quietly over the weekend."

Massey felt stunned. They knew. That meant the nuclear bomb and terrorist attacks were planned and coordinated by most of the countries outside NATO. And if the diplomats were gone, then downtown Washington, DC, was no longer off limits to attack.

"Call the Cabinet and Joint Chiefs," Massey ordered, running a hand through his hair in frustration. "I want everyone back in the Situation Room in one hour."

"Yes, Sir," Jenkins said as he backed out of the room.

North Carolina, USA

Ginny woke early as usual. She dressed then went downstairs and started the coffee. She was pouring herself a cup when Pete joined her. He poured a cup of his own and sat beside her at the kitchen island.

"Sleep well?" he asked.

"Um hmm," she mumbled, still looking at her coffee. "Did you?"

He grinned and repeated her mumble, "Um hmm."

Ginny shoved him playfully with her shoulder. "You know I mumble until I have coffee."

"Do I?" he asked.

"Don't you?"

"I don't remember," he said. "I don't think I saw that in the dream."

"Well now you know," Ginny said. "I am incoherent until I have that jolt of caffeine."

"Now I know," he said with a slightly crooked smile.

"What's on your agenda today?" she asked.

"Garrett and his boys were supposed to get the cameras downloaded and running smoothly last night. I want to see how they work. Max, Sharon, and I are going to check in with our crews across the nation. So far, they're all safe. Then I guess we can go see your neighbor, Aaron, later today."

Mark came into the kitchen.

"How's the cow?"

"She'll be fine," Ginny said. "I predict she will even have more calves. Mark, Tom Sutton has placed game cameras all over his farm. I don't think he had a dream, but he said that something told him he needed to do that and soon. He bought more Monday. He said he and Brady spent the day getting them placed and running. His son, Jerry, was on his way home from Charlotte on the tenth and hasn't arrived. Tom thinks he got caught in traffic and ran out of gas. This is one time I hope the dreams are right and that boy gets home safely."

"Interesting," Mark said. "Bob had a dream, Tom had a premonition, and Aaron had nothing. I wonder what the common denominator is among the people who received some type of warning."

"Only God knows that Mark," Ginny said.

"True." Mark turned when he heard the stampede of the boys running up the stairs from the basement and the giggles of the girls padding down the stairs from the second floor. He whistled at the pack of children that flooded into the kitchen.

"Inside commotion, please," he said.

Ginny put out cereal and bowls for the children then looked at the menu so she could start prepping breakfast.

Brad came out of the office while everyone was getting breakfast. He grabbed a plate and got in line behind Garrett.

"What are your plans today?" Garrett asked.

"I need to plant corn." Brad answered, spooning eggs onto his plate. "Want to help?"

"I would love to," Garrett replied, grabbing a piece of toast. "It's been a while. I miss being here and the physical act of planting a crop. It's satisfying work."

"Well, let's get you reacquainted with the chore," Brad said smiling. After breakfast, he and Garrett walked to the barn.

Brad always liked working in the fields; he did some of his best thinking on the tractor. He glanced out of the tractor cab at Garrett. The guy had to be bored, then Brad noticed the book in his brother's hand. He smiled. He couldn't remember a time when Garrett wasn't reading unless he was doing something that required both hands.

Brad pulled up to the truck. Garrett set the book aside and slipped off the tailgate. With practiced ease, he refilled the hoppers with corn seed. The sight tugged at Brad's memory, riding in the cab as a little boy with his father and watching a teenage Garrett do the same job for their dad. Brad smiled and started another row of corn.

At noon they stopped for the quick lunch Garrett had brought, and then Brad went back to planting. He was almost finished with the field when he stopped, pulled the tractor up to the truck and turned off the engine.

"I've finished the corn," Brad said as he got out of the tractor cab. "I want to change out the hopper and plant the rest of the field in the sweet corn seeds I bought last week. We'll need a lot more than we usually put in the garden."

"That's good thinking, Brad." Garrett said. "I'll follow you back to the barn. Do you want to take care of that planting today?"

"Yes," Brad answered. "It won't hurt anything to go ahead and plant. We still have another week or so for the danger of frost, but I don't think the plants will be up yet."

Garrett followed Brad back to the barn, helped him change hoppers and followed him back to the corn field. Brad had the sweet corn planted in thirty minutes, and the two drove back to the house.

"Thanks for helping and bringing the lunch, Garrett," Brad said when all the equipment was back in the shed. "Do you think people are starting to wonder why Holly isn't here?"

"Remember the plan," Garrett said. "If anyone asks, tell them the truth. Holly didn't believe you about bad times coming and chose to stay in Elkin. The dreams have changed in other ways, it can change that way too."

"You're right," Brad said, nodding. "With every day that passes, I realize more what a poor match we would have been. I'm beginning to be relieved that it ended the way it did."

"Now that is the sound of wisdom." Garrett said as he clapped his hand against Brad's shoulder, and they walked back to the house.

Pete and Ginny finished lunch and were getting ready to go to the Johnson farm. They passed Adam, Brett, and Michael standing in the yard where they were testing their drone. Ginny looked up to see it buzzing over the barn.

Pete looked at the display on their tablet. "Wow, those are some great pictures."

"Watch the display," Brett said. He pushed some buttons, and the drone flew south. He pointed to a road on the screen. "That's highway 421."

"That's amazing," Pete said. "How far away is that highway, fifteen miles?"

"Close" Ginny said. "I think it is nearer to twenty. I'm impressed that the drone can go that far."

"Look at the traffic," Pete said, pointing to the screen. "It looks like it's bumper to bumper still."

"It's day three," Ginny said. "Isn't that when most people start to panic? It looks like the west bound side has more traffic than the east bound side. People must be trying to get out of Winston and Greensboro. I hope those people have a destination to go to in the mountains and they aren't just fleeing with the hope of finding refuge."

"Can you show me the farm south of here?" Pete asked Brett. "I've seen satellite pictures, but I want to see it in real time."

Brett moved his drone over to the Johnson farm. Pete saw the house and all the buildings, the pastures and the cattle.

"Thanks," he said and turned to Ginny. "Does Aaron know we're coming?"

"Yes," she said, pulling out her keys. "I just called him. We can take my work truck. This is a follow-up visit for me."

Ginny pulled out the driveway, turned south, then almost immediately turned into the Johnson's farm.

"You weren't kidding," Pete said, taking his first look at the property. "That house is very close to the road, closer than I thought it was in the dream."

Ginny drove around the house and to the horse barn. Bonnie came out of the barn and met her.

"Hey Miss Ginny," she said. "Star and Sunshine are doing well."

"You named her Sunshine?" Ginny asked, smiling. "I like it."

Aaron walked up.

"Aaron," Ginny said, "this is Pete Flinn. He's a friend of Mark's and the security specialist I was telling you about."

"It's nice to meet you, Mr. Johnson," Pete said as he extended his hand.

"Please call me Aaron," he said and shook Pete's hand. "It's nice to meet you too. I'm grateful for any advice you can give me."

Aaron watched Bonnie and Ginny go into the barn.

"Donna and I went to Elkin yesterday," he said to Pete, looking around to make sure they were alone. "Things are tense. The shelves are pretty bare now, and there seems to be a sleezy crowd running around town, causing trouble, and intimidating people into giving up their supplies."

"Blue pickup?" Pete asked, thinking about the truck in the dream.

"That's the one. Have you seen it?" Aaron asked.

"Only from a distance," Pete said, amazed at the accuracy of the dream. "I looked at your aerial photo on the internet and one of the boys at the farm flew his drone over your place."

"That must be what I heard a few minutes ago," Aaron said. "Carson has one for monitoring the cows, so I know what they sound like. Come into the barn. I have an office in the back, and we can talk."

Pete followed Aaron into his office and studied the records and photos spread across the desk. They began to make a plan. Pete recommended game cameras and moving the animals as far back on the property as he could.

"Aaron," Pete said, frowning as he met the man's eyes. "I can't do anything about your house; it's very close to the road. I recommend moving your valuables and a good portion of your supplies to that barn on the north side. They'll be safer there if someone tries to break in or steal from you."

"I thought that's what you would say," Aaron sighed. "I've been moving tools and feed there already. Carson and I will start moving things faster. I really doubt anything will happen, but I never expected nuclear missiles and terrorist bombs, either. That barn has an apartment in the loft. I built it in so I could keep tabs on new foals. It will be a safe place to store our valuables for a while."

"Sounds like a good plan," Pete said. He and Aaron walked back out to the truck.

Ginny came out of the barn and said, "Aaron, those horses look good. You and Bonnie take good care of your animals. I appreciate that."

They all turned around when an SUV came up the driveway. It stopped and a woman got out of the driver's side. Donna ran out of the house toward the woman and hugged her tightly. Bonnie ran out of the barn and pulled open the back door, grabbing the teenage girl inside.

"That's Donna's older sister, Grace," Aaron said to Ginny and Pete. "She teaches in Huntersville. Donna talked with her the day of the bombings, and they were planning to come up here. It's only a two-hour drive, but we hadn't heard from her since. Donna's been worried sick."

Another woman got out of the passenger's seat and watched the reunion.

"Bonnie's hugging Hannah, Grace's daughter," Aaron explained. "I don't know the other woman."

Donna brought Grace and Hannah over to introduce them to Ginny and Pete. Grace took the other woman's hand and pulled her into the group.

"This is my friend and neighbor, Tina Koontz," Grace said. "She's a first-year math teacher at the high school where I teach English. Hannah and I were getting ready to leave yesterday when I saw her standing outside her condo. I couldn't just leave her there. I helped her pack and brought her with us. Donna, I hope you don't mind."

"Tina, it's nice to meet you," Donna said, "and you are welcome here. Grace, you did the right thing. You couldn't leave a young woman on her own in the city during this time."

"Thank you so much Mr. and Mrs. Johnson," Tina said.

"Call me Donna," she said and pointed at Aaron. "And you can call him Aaron."

"Tina, I'm glad you're here," Aaron said, giving her a nod. "I would hate to think of a nice person like you alone in a crisis like this."

Tears welled in Tina's eyes as she looked at the Johnson's.

"Thank you so much." She looked at Grace. "Thank you. I've never been so scared. The power was out, and no one knew what was going on."

"I was scared, too," Grace said as she put her arm around Tina. "We're safe now." Grace looked at Donna and Aaron. "Because we changed plans, we didn't leave until after lunch. It normally takes us two hours to get here, but when I saw the bumper to bumper traffic on I-77, I didn't even try to get on the interstate. We took the back roads.

"I thought we could get past Statesville before dark, but we couldn't. It was slow getting around Cornelius and Davidson. When we got to Mooresville, it was already getting dark. I stopped to get gas, and the owner of the gas station warned us to get off the road and continue this morning. He had already seen fights over gas and supplies and thought it would get worse after dark. He let us park behind his station until this morning.

"We started again after the sun came up, and it still took us this long to get here. It was slow-going at first, but the farther north we got, the more the traffic thinned out. Once we got past Hwy 421, we were able to get around Elkin and up here without any trouble."

Grace looked at Donna and Aaron. "Thank you so much for letting us come. I don't think we would've survived if we'd stayed. Charlotte was getting dangerous. We heard those bombs all the way in Huntersville. People were fleeing the city, trying to get out before things got worse. A neighbor told us gangs were already taking over and fighting each other for territory.

"Then there was the smoke. We could barely breath outside because the air was so thick with smoke and dust from the explosions. By yesterday morning, dust coated my car, like it had snowed overnight. Fires were still burning. Buildings, gasoline tanks, natural gas lines, and the smoke just kept spreading. The fire departments and police stations downtown were destroyed with equipment and personnel trapped inside. No one could respond to anything.

"The bombs exploded water mains and sewers. Contaminated water was running down the streets. Even the homes that weren't damaged weren't safe because of the air pollution, contaminated water, no electricity, and no way to fix it quickly. It's a nightmare, and there's no one left to help. That's why there are so many people leaving."

"I'm glad you're not there now, Grace," Aaron said reassuringly. "Family sticks together. We wanted you to come, and we're glad you brought Tina. We have to do our best to take care of each other now."

"We need to get back," Ginny said, looking at Pete then back to the others. "Grace, it's nice to meet you and Tina."

"It's nice to meet you, Grace," Pete said. "You were wise to leave Charlotte so quickly. We're glad you made it here safely."

Pete and Ginny left the Johnson family standing in their yard.

"What did Aaron say?" Ginny asked when they got in the truck.

"He understands the danger of living so close to the road. He's already moving feed and tools to the back of the farm. He's really worried about his kids, and now there's another teenage girl in the house. Did you know his barn on the north side of the farm has a small apartment above it instead of a full loft?"

"I hadn't known that until my dream," Ginny answered.

"Ginny," Pete said, "Aaron gave me some details about their trip to Elkin yesterday. They stopped at the discount store, and the Larkin boys and their friends were in the parking lot harassing people as they came out of the store, especially women. That was the tipping point for Donna. Now she's focused on securing their home and making sure they have adequate supplies.

"He also said Elkin has turned into a ghost town. No one is on the streets, and the police are patrolling everywhere. Theft and looting have already started. He said they went to that upscale grocery store on the north side of the town. It's almost empty, and the prices have more than doubled."

"And that was just day two," Ginny said, letting her head fall back against the headrest and closing her eyes. "It's crazy how fast this has all happened."

Leah had just prepped for dinner, sliding three large casseroles into the ovens when the lights flickered and the power went out.

"Don't panic," she said calmly, reassuring the little girls sitting at the breakfast nook. "The generator is working. Besides, if I remember correctly, the power comes back on shortly."

Fifteen minutes later, the lights flickered back on, and the generator quieted.

"Power restored," Leah said.

"That's probably the first of multiple blackouts to come," Barbara commented.

"How are we doing?" Ginny asked as she came into the kitchen. "Is everything all right?"

"Perfect," Leah answered. "Your generator worked like a charm. I have the boys checking the internet to see if there's a reason for the outage."

During dinner, Adam reported they couldn't find any information online about the power outages. Mark asked about the Johnsons, and Pete explained that their house had definite security risks. They were already moving supplies and valuables to the barn on the north side of their farm, just in case.

"While we were there," Ginny said, "Donna's sister, Grace, drove up with her daughter Hannah and a neighbor, Tina Koontz. They left Charlotte yesterday afternoon and took back roads the whole way. It was slow going. They slept in the car behind a gas station last night and got to Aaron's today without trouble. They said Charlotte feels like a war zone with rival gangs fighting over territory and supplies. I don't think those three would have survived if they had stayed."

Ginny remembered that Tina had been attractive, petite with curly light brown hair and green eyes. She glanced at Brad. He was eating, staring down at his plate, and not making eye contact with anyone. She didn't think he was even listening to the conversation and wondered whether he and Tina might end up becoming friends.

Ginny looked at Garrett, who sat next to her.

"Garrett," Ginny said softly, "Grace changed the dream. She brought Tina with her. Tina wasn't with her in my dream."

Garrett thought for a moment. "You're right. I can only assume that something else changed and opened a place for Tina to come to their farm. Maybe something was different in Charlotte."

Ginny nodded and looked at Garrett. She knew they were both thinking the same thing. The main difference was that Holly wasn't at the farm.

Adam sat quietly at the table looking at the internet on his phone.

"Hey," he said, standing. "Somebody turn on the TV. I think we retaliated against North Korea."

Robert turned the television on and switched to the Winston-Salem station. The news anchor's voice was tight, sounding concerned about the latest news.

"Overnight in Asia, the U.S. launched a coordinated strike on the Korean Peninsula. Large attack drones slipped in low, under the radar, and fired missiles that destroyed several of North Korea's nuclear-weapon silos. Another wave hit a remote plutonium production facility, a blow analysts say would cripple the country's nuclear program. All targets were deep in isolated terrain. No cities. No civilian centers. The President and Secretary of Defense are waiting on a report from officers on the ground in South Korea as to the damage inside North Korea and any early signs as to how the regime might respond."

"Just like the dreams," Garrett said. "I guess we wait and see what happens."

"I wonder if North Korea or China will retaliate," Alex said. "We know what happened in the dreams, but it will be interesting to see if their response stays the same."

CHAPTER 14

APRIL 13

Switzerland

The Committee met again at the Rosen estate in response to the U.S. retaliation against North Korea. Mr. Lin from China was angry. He looked at Rosen.

"We were assured that your man in America would keep them from attacking North Korea," Lin said curtly. "Now, a plume of radioactive air from the plutonium plant is drifting toward China."

John Rosen took a deep breath, trying to control his own emotions. After months of working with him, he had discovered Lin's short, volatile temper.

"Mr. Lin," John said calmly, "as we discussed before, we expected some type of retaliation from the United States. Mr. Miller did well to keep it small with only drone attacks. Bombing the plutonium production plant was unexpected, but it's still better than a nuclear attack. If a radioactive plume is heading toward China, then you need to address the positioning of the plant with the North Korean government."

Rosen looked at the other men and women in the room. He reassured them that everything was still on schedule.

"I think that's all for now," he said. "We will meet again tomorrow morning. If my information from the Federal Reserve is correct, we can expect an even more dramatic plunge in the Dow Jones Average. It should close the stock market for several days."

Hiding a smile, Rosen stood as the participants left the conference room. George stood just inside the door, watching until they were gone.

"George," John said, "I think we should have them followed. What's your opinion?"

"I agree," George said. "Our people are in place to see where they go, who they talk to, and find out what they say. Our timeline is at a point too critical to get blindsided by one of the countries going back on their agreement."

"You're right," John replied. "They will eventually start to suspect each other as they realize things are happening without their knowledge, then we make sure they turn on each other. But we don't want them to get to that point yet." John stood, "Let's go downstairs. We have our own plans to make."

George followed Rosen to an elevator which took them down from the main floor, below the basement, and to a much lower level. When the door opened, they walked into an underground bunker complete with electricity, food storage, access to water, and a completely hardened, off-grid communication room.

⸻◆○◆⸻

North Carolina, USA

Ginny woke early. Instead of trying to go back to sleep, she got dressed and headed downstairs. It was her day to fix breakfast, and she figured she could get a head start.

When she got to the kitchen, she found Pete in the den staring at the computer. She poured heself a cup of coffee and slid into the chair beside him. Only then did she noticed the images filling the screen.

"Are those from the game cameras?" she asked.

"Yes," Pete answered. "We'll start monitoring them today, but I wanted to get a feel for how to keep watch on so many pictures at the same time. It's not bad. It's enough to keep from getting bored but not so many you can't see them on one monitor."

"Look here," Pete said, pointing to one picture. "There's a doe with her fawn. I've been watching them wander the property."

"Wow, that's a really good picture," Ginny said. "It's so clear you can count the spots on the fawn."

"It'll make identification of people and vehicles easier," he said. "No fuzzy images."

Ginny stood. "It's my turn to make breakfast. If you get tired of watching nature TV, you can keep me company."

Pete chuckled as he left the computer.

"We may as well listen to the news," he said from the den.

Pete turned the television to the Winston-Salem channel. The news showed footage of people stranded along the interstates across the nation, living in their cars or tents where they ran out of gas. Most had been trying to leave the cities due to rising crime and dwindling supplies. The Red Cross and local municipalities were trying to help as much as they could, but it was turning into a humanitarian crisis.

"That's awful," Ginny said. "Those poor people."

"I've seen this before in other countries," Pete said. "War creates refugees. This will get worse."

The others had come downstairs and were watching the news.

"Any word about North Korea?" Alex asked.

"Not yet," Pete said. "But they could have reported it before I turned on the TV."

The television was turned off when the smaller children came in for breakfast. The adults sat around the table eating and planning the day. Pete handed out the rotation schedule for monitoring the game camera pictures on the computer. Brett had the honor of the first two-hour shift. They were discussing the outhouse and shower when Ginny's phone rang.

"This is Dr. Reed." The group quietly listened to Ginny.

"Hey Tom." After a pause, Ginny exclaimed, "What! Oh no! I was afraid of that. Could you see who it was on your game cameras?" Ginny listened. "Do you think so? Yeah, Brad and I will be right over to help you do that. See you in a few minutes."

Ginny looked at the group. "Tom Sutton's steer was butchered last night, exactly like in the dream. His game cameras caught something, but the image was fuzzy. If he had to guess, he thinks it might have been a sheriff's deputy, Dwight Hall, and another man." She turned to Mark. "That's who it was in the dream."

Brad and Ginny rode four wheelers across their pastures to Tom's farm. Tom waited on the far side of the barbed wire fence, wire cutters in hand. Ginny saw the gap he had made to allow his cows to cross into their pasture, which was farther from the road and harder for anyone to reach.

Brad and Ginny eased the herd forward with their vehicles, nudging the cows toward the opening. Tom and Brady funneled the cows through the gap. When the last cow stepped into Ginny's pasture, Tom closed the opening and refastened the fencing.

"I really appreciate this," Tom said as he shook hands with Ginny and Brad. "We can't stand to lose any more cows. Who knows how long all this will last, and we may end up having to eat every single one of them."

"No worries, Tom," Brad said reassuringly. "Glad to do it. I own the Thompson place now, so we can even use some of those empty pastures."

Tom smiled. "I didn't know that! Congratulations on your purchase. You got good land."

"I know," Brad said. "I'm pretty happy about it." He hesitated before shifting gears. "Tom, were you able to see who killed your steer? Ginny said you have game cameras up."

"I should have," Tom said. "There were two men, but they were at just the right angle that my cameras didn't get a good shot. If I had to guess, I'm almost certain one of them was Dwight Hall. He doesn't live far from here and is probably too lazy to garden or hunt food legally. I don't know why the sheriff keeps him on."

"I agree," Brad said. "I'm afraid Dwight may be trouble." He paused again. "Tom, the Speaks and the Millers keep cows in pastures near the road, don't they?"

"Yes, they do," Tom replied. "I need to call them and tell them to move their livestock out of sight. I wish I'd done that for my own cows before now."

"That's a good idea," Brad said. "If this keeps up, it's just a matter of time before someone gets hurt trying to stop the thieves."

Brad and Ginny returned to their farm. When they parked their four wheelers in the shed, Brad told Ginny about his conversation with Tom.

"I hope Tom follows through and calls the Speaks and Millers," he said. "If so, it may keep both of those men from getting shot like they did in the dream." He noticed Ginny had not looked up from her phone. "Who do you keep texting?"

"Jacque," Ginny said. "I told her to come, and she's trying to get here. She's safe, but she's been working as a doctor the whole way and keeps getting stopped. Right now, she's staying at a home to deliver a baby."

"Well, I hope she gets here. A human doctor would be nice to have around," he said grinning.'

"You can make fun all you want. I just want her here," Ginny said, sounding worried.

Brad wrapped an arm around Ginny's shoulders. "That woman is as smart and resilient as you are. She'll get here."

Tina Koontz was tired. She had spent the day helping the Johnsons move their supplies and valuables to the apartment above the back barn. Tomorrow, she would be in the garden, working with the cool-season plants.

It was getting late, and she still hadn't fallen asleep. The house was quiet. She was lying under a well-worn quilt on the sofa bed in the living room, and for the first time in days, she felt like she could take a deep breath without panicking. Her mind kept circling back to the dream she had last week, before everything fell apart. She had been on a farm. Not this one, but maybe the farm in the dream was more symbolic than literal.

Because of that dream, she'd gone shopping over the weekend, buying every winter item she could still find, along with spring and summer clothes, shoes, underwear, toiletries, and over-the-counter remedies. She'd packed everything neatly, ready to leave at a moment's notice, then Grace offered to take her with them.

She thought of her family. Her brother, sister and parents lived on the family farm in rural southern Virginia. She was grateful they were together, but she knew they were worried about her. She'd called to let them know she was safe, but there was no way she could get to them. The roads had been too clogged, too dangerous. She still couldn't believe how harrowing the trip here had been.

A tear slid down her cheek and onto the pillowcase. She felt displaced, out of place, and anxious. She was alone among strangers, and even though they were nice, they were still strangers. Tina turned over, buried her head into the pillow and cried herself to sleep.

CHAPTER 15

APRIL 14

Switzerland

John Rosen and George Thomas sat at the dining room table in the chalet, eating lunch. George updated John on the situation in America.

"Our people struck again during the night in the United States," George said. "They targeted new cities and re-hit some of the cities that were damaged during the first wave. Residents are extremely nervous because nowhere feels safe. We also detonated bombs in a number of small rural towns. No dirty bombs, though. The natural resources are still intact.

"According to the media in the United States, there's widespread panic. Rioting and looting in the cities have increased. Refugees are clogging the interstates as they try to escape populated areas. We've seen video footage of stranded travelers robbing other travelers. Houses along the outbound roads are being looted and burned. Supply lines are breaking down, a black market is emerging, the dollar is nearly worthless, and inflation is spiraling out of control."

"Excellent," John said. "Just like we wanted." He studied George for a moment. "I think it's time we sent our young American friend back to his boss. From this point on, Mr. Miller needs to be kept in the dark. He's served his purpose."

John smiled. "Let's send him home. Then we'll wait a few days before we drop some hints in Washington that Jacob Miller knew about the attacks and that he's been receiving payment for his services." He leaned in slightly. "Can we be sure that nothing can be traced back to us, even if Jacob Miller confesses to everything?"

"I'll take care of the young Mr. Becker today," George said, smiling. He didn't like the arrogant man, even though he knew John did.

"He should be back in the United States by tomorrow morning," George said confidently. "Also, be assured, if anyone investigates Jacob Miller, they will find that his information about the attacks and payment for his services came from shadow government accounts in China, Russia, and Iran."

"Excellent," Rosen replied. "How close are we to being ready for the next phase?"

"Soon," George replied. "The technicians in the bunker are still working on getting into the computer networks of the military and upper levels of the governments of both the United States and China. The other countries have already been accessed."

Rosen gave a small smile. "Let me know when everything is ready."

George nodded.

◆○◆

North Carolina, USA

Brad woke up early again after another poor night's sleep. Hoping coffee would help, he walked into the kitchen and poured himself a large cup. Thanks to the dreams, they were able to stock up on it, but the supply would not last forever. He dreaded the day they would actually run out of it.

He stepped into the den and stopped beside the couch where Ginny sat watching the television.

"The terrorists struck again," Ginny said shaking her head. "Just like in the dream, only worse. They hit Wichita, St. Louis, Dallas, New Orleans, Spokane, Reno, Chicago and Boston. They also destroyed two power plants in the northeast, not nuclear. What wasn't in the dream was how many small towns were hit. That really set off a panic. Now, no one feels safe anywhere."

"Someone, somewhere, must really hate us," Brad said sadly as he shook his head and sat down beside her to watch the news.

Breakfast was served, and Brad ate quietly, not interacting with the group. He got up and started to take his plate to the sink when he heard that an unknown pickup was seen on the monitor. He didn't stay to listen. Security was not his responsibility, farming and food were. He had a lot of people to feed and a lot of work to get done.

Brad started the smallest tractor on the farm and went to the garden plot. One area already had lettuce, onions, and cabbages ready for picking. He prepared the rest of the garden for planting and enlarged it to three times the normal size. It now covered an entire acre and a half. He hoped it would be enough. If necessary, he could start another garden later in the summer to plant cool season food.

With that finished, Brad, Mike, Robert, Max, Garrett and Alex rode to Brad's farm to start building the pole barn. Before they started on the barn, they helped Brad board up the doors and windows on the front of the farmhouse. Brad hoped it would deter anyone from trying to break in. By the time the men came back to the house for dinner, the poles had been set and the framing started. They would easily finish the next day.

Washington, DC

Donald Evans was tired. His offices at the Pentagon were unusable, and he was relegated to a small, windowless space in the interior of the West Wing of the White House. He could live with that. What he was having trouble with was the way President Massey kept relying on Jacob Miller, the National Security Advisor. No matter what anyone recommended to the President, he always took Miller's advice. Miller would have them sit on their hands and do nothing while the terrorists continued to wreak havoc on the country.

Evans felt his stomach growl and looked at his watch. It was after 6:00 pm. Sighing, he closed his laptop and packed everything into his briefcase. He needed food, and he could finish his work from home.

After stopping at his condo to drop off his briefcase and change out of his work clothes, Evans walked to a small sports bar near his home. He was grateful the place was still open. Sliding into a booth, he immediately ordered a burger, fries and a beer. He leaned his head against the high seat back and sighed.

His quiet reverie was disrupted when he felt his seat shift beneath him as someone slid into the booth behind him. The person was on the phone, and he didn't even need to look to know who it was. It was Jacob Miller. The bar was quiet, so Evans just listened.

"Yes, John, everything here is under control," Miller said in a low tone. "The terrorists are very successful, and the President is in a state of complete indecision. This is perfect for the plan because the President is listening to everything I tell him and not listening to any of this other advisors. But not only that, the Vice President, Cabinet, and Congressional Leaders are paralyzed because they keep getting conflicting reports."

Miller was quiet for a moment. The waiter brought Donald's food.

Not wanting Miller to hear his voice, Donald smiled his thanks and took a sip of his beer.

"Don't worry, John," Miller continued. "Between the terrorist attacks, stock market crash, and riots, the military is too busy keeping control of their own citizens under martial law. They won't be watching the rest of the world. I've almost convinced Massey to recall our troops from Europe and Asia to protect the homeland. Once that happens, you'll have free reign to take the territory you want."

Miller listened for a moment. "I'll keep you posted." After a few more murmured comments, the call ended.

Evans stared at his food as his appetite disappeared. Fury simmered in his chest. He was angry with himself for not getting his cell phone out in time to record the most important part of conversation, which proved Miller's treachery. He was furious with Miller because it sounded like the man was working with someone to bring about the downfall of the United States for a larger agenda somewhere in the world. What infuriated him even more were Miller's last comments before ending the call, that all bonuses were appreciated. The man was guilty of treason.

Evans was glad he had not revealed his presence, but he had no idea how to proceed. He didn't want Miller to know that his conversation had been heard, so he sat quietly in the dim light of the bar, forcing himself to eat, and waiting to pay his bill only after Miller left.

North Carolina, USA

After dinner, Brad got his fishing pole out of the storage closet in the basement and headed outside to go to the stocked pond that sat on his new farm. He was walking across the yard to his truck when he heard his name called from the back door. The boys wanted to go along.

He smiled and went back to the house to get extra fishing poles. The boys rode in the back of the truck across the farm paths to the pond, excited for an adventure. Soon, they were unloading the truck and baiting their hooks.

"What's in the pond?" Michael asked as he cast his line into the water.

"I don't know," Brad answered. "I just bought this place. Mr. Thompson said it was stocked, but he didn't say with what type of fish."

"I hope it's catfish," Adam said. "I like salt and pepper catfish."

In less than a minute, Brad felt his line tug, and he reeled in the fish.

"Adam, you get your wish," Brad said. "This is a small catfish. I hope the rest are bigger."

"I got one!" Michael yelled as he reeled in a slightly larger catfish.

Before Brad and Michael could rebait their hooks, Adam, Caleb, Bobby and Brett had each caught a fish. Brad let the boys continue to fish while he started a line on which to string them.

When they had ten fish, Brad said, "That's enough. Let's not deplete the stock, although it might be overcrowded in there since we caught so many so quickly. That means we can come back and fish again soon."

It was getting dark when Brad parked his truck by the barn. The boys ran into the house, bragging to their parents about their fishing expertise. Brad followed, smiling at their enthusiasm.

"Okay, guys," he said. "It's time to clean them."

Brad took the boys out to the barn where he had a table that he used to clean fish whenever he and his buddies went fishing at a local river or fly fishing in a mountain trout stream. He showed the boys how to scrape, gut, and fillet the catfish. He placed the fillets in a plastic food container and took it to Leah. She placed them in the refrigerator to add to the next night's dinner.

Brad followed what had become a nightly routine for him. He showered and closed himself inside the office where he watched a movie until he fell asleep.

CHAPTER 16

APRIL 15

North Carolina, USA

Looking for breakfast, Brad entered the kitchen to find Ginny, Pete and Bennett at the computer, studying the monitor intensely. They pointed at the screen, discussing the same black pickup they had seen the day before. It was back and had stopped at the Smith farm. As he placed his breakfast plate on the table, he watched Garrett leave the house to get into Aaron Johnson's truck. Evidently, they were going to make sure that it was some of the Smith family taking refuge at that farmhouse. That's who it had been in the dream.

After breakfast, Brad and the other men drove back to his farm to finish the pole barn. By the end of the day, it stood completed. Brad thanked his friends; it was the fastest he had ever seen one of those structures built.

After dinner, Garrett filled him in on the Smith family moving into the old farmhouse. As he got ready for bed, Brad realized he really didn't care about the Smith family, and his indifference made him feel strangely guilty. He knew his disconnect was temporary and just his way of dealing with the stress of their new lives and the sting of Holly's rejection. He reminded himself to be patient, that he would get back to normal. He didn't like the version of himself that he currently was. He was ready to be his old self, and that, he realized, was a good sign.

———◈———

Washington, DC

It was early afternoon when Greg Becker knocked on Jacob Miller's office door. He was nervous about meeting face to face with his boss. He should still be in Switzerland. Greg had been their only link to the decisions being made by the Committee. Now, there was no way they could know what was happening unless John Rosen chose to tell them.

"Enter," Miller said.

Greg entered the office and said, "Mr. Miller."

Jacob Miller looked up from his paperwork, his eyes widening in surprise. "Greg? What are you doing here?"

Greg gave Miller an apologetic look. "I was sent home. George, John Rosen's assistant, had my things packed for me at the hotel then escorted me to the airport with a one way ticket to Freeport. A fast boat brought me to the yacht club and a car took me home. It happened fast, and I was constantly watched. I didn't have time to make a private call to you."

"Why?" Miller asked incredulously. "I mean, why did they send you home?"

"I don't know," Greg said, shaking his head. "Could we walk, Sir?"

Miller nodded. They needed to talk on the grounds as far away from surveillance equipment as possible. After getting coffee from the break room, the two walked out onto the lawn.

"Tell me," Miller said.

"Sir," Greg said, "I think we served our purpose with The Committee. The United States has pretty much had her wings clipped, so to speak. They don't fear us anymore. I think they sent me home to keep us in the dark as to what's going to happen next."

Miller nodded. "Did they tell you that all the diplomats from non-NATO countries have left Washington?"

Greg's head snapped up in shock; his eyes widened.

"No! I didn't know that!" Greg said incredulously.

"I'm afraid I agree with you," Miller said, sighing in frustration. "If we are no longer useful to The Committee, I don't know what they're capable of doing. Tie up your loose ends. Don't pack anything. We'll plan on leaving tonight. Air traffic is still grounded, so we can't use the jet. I've had other arrangements made, just in case. It will take a lot longer, but we'll still get to Belize. We can live a long time on the estate without having to leave. Thank goodness my wife and daughter are already there."

"Yes, Sir," Greg said. "I'll be ready."

That evening, Jacob Miller and Greg Becker met at a high-end Mexican restaurant that was somehow still open in Georgetown despite the looted stores around it. After a quick meal, they slipped out the back door and climbed into the back of a delivery van. Inside, they changed into jeans, t-shirts, hoodies, and ball caps.

An hour later, the van stopped at a residence in Virginia. The driver of the van tossed them a set of keys to an older pickup truck parked in the driveway then held a paper bag out the window. Greg opened it and found two new cell phones, a large envelope of cash, and a road map.

Two hours later, they were winding along roads through rural North Carolina on their way to Miami. Once there, a yacht would take them to Nassau, where a charter jet waited to fly Jacob and Greg to Belize.

Chapter 17

April 16

Brad walked into the kitchen for coffee and breakfast. He heard the group discussing the man they saw walking down the road in the middle of the night. It turned out to be Jerry Sutton, Tom's son, who had finally gotten home from Charlotte. However, in the dreams he had been alone. This time he brought a young woman with him, holding her hand as they walked. They assumed she was his girlfriend.

Suddenly, alerts chimed from all the phones in the kitchen. Brad opened the news site, and his anxiety ticked upward.

Ginny scanned her feed and read aloud.

"North Korea started bombing Seoul, then they invaded," she read. "South Korea responded by bombing Pyongyang. North Korea bombed our military base in the south, and South Korea bombed a military airfield in the north. Those poor people."

Everyone was discussing the latest news, escalating terrorist attacks, and global warfare, wondering what it meant for them on the farm. Brad stood apart from the group, looking out the kitchen window. The weather had shifted, and the wind was blowing slightly harder from the west.

As he thought about how their isolation could keep them safe, he noticed the wind was bringing smoke and dust from the bombed cities. If it grew thick enough, it could block sunlight and lower temperatures, threatening their ability to grow food. He sighed. There was nothing they could do but wait and see what happened in the coming days.

Brad heard footsteps on the stairs and turned to see Garrett coming into the kitchen. He walked up to Brad.

"Can we talk?" Garrett asked.

"Sure. What's up?" Brad asked.

Garrett led him to the end of the kitchen next to the office.

"It's Sunday," Garrett said. "I think it would be good to have a church service like we did in the dream, especially considering the recent news."

"That's a good idea," Brad said. "Where do you want to set it up?"

Mark came over. "What are we talking about?"

"Church," Garrett said.

"Why not do it outside," Brad said, gesturing past the back door. "The weather's decent. We can rearrange the picnic tables and set up yard chairs in a semicircle; Garrett can speak from the center."

"I like it," Garrett said.

Ginny walked over and asked, "Can I get in this conversation?"

"We're discussing church," Garrett said, putting his arm around Ginny's shoulders. "Brad's going to set things up outside while I make an announcement.

"That sounds good," she said. "I have extra chairs in the attic if we need them."

After breakfast, Mark and Brad arranged the lawn chairs in the backyard. Garrett made the announcement to the others, and soon everyone was outside listening to Garrett read scripture. He discussed how they should work hard and do everything they could to survive while remembering that it is God who is in control, which means work but don't worry.

Brad thought Garrett had a good way of explaining faith and was perfect for this role.

Mark declared the day one of rest and relaxation, just as a Sunday should be. Adults read, talked, and wandered the farm. The kids played corn hole and other outdoor games. Max and Adam worked with Brute and Barf.

Brad sat in a chair at the edge of the yard, watching the activity but feeling disconnected and off balance. After a few minutes, he stood, walked to the equipment shed, got in the golf cart and quietly slipped away down the path to his own farm.

He had owned the house for two weeks, but had never taken the time to walk through it. Other than memories of the front rooms from visiting the Thompsons, he didn't even know the complete layout of it. He had bought the place sight unseen.

He parked the cart and stepped into a screened porch that stretched across the entire back of the house. It was mostly empty except for a large table and a couple of rocking chairs. He went through the back door into a long hallway. A bathroom stood on the left, a kitchen on the right, both closed off by doors. Older homes didn't have open layouts.

Brad opened the door to the kitchen. An electric range was on the right, and beside it stood an unplugged refrigerator, open and still smelling faintly of bleach. He noticed there was no dishwasher, which didn't bother him. In the opposite corner, a wood burning cookstove stood on an old hearth with a flue running up the chimney. He smiled. He loved those old stoves. He would have to experiment with this one.

A door beside the cookstove opened into the dining room. A fireplace stood on the same wall as the kitchen's wood stove, giving Brad the idea that it might be easy to heat this area in the winter. He crossed the dining room and stepped into the front hallway. Past the front door, he found a family room the same size as the dining room with a fireplace on the wall shared with the next room. The family room was clean, and the Thompsons had left their living room furniture.

Back in the hallway, he circled around the stairwell to the bathroom. It had once been a full room of the original house, complete with a window and fireplace. Cabinets and shelves lined one wall for storage.

Upstairs, Brad walked through three bedrooms and a separate bathroom. To his delight, every room had a fireplace. At the back of the house, he stepped into a sunporch built above the downstairs porch. The afternoon sun poured in, and he knew it would catch the evening light as well. It would be a wonderful place in the winter.

Brad went back down the stairs and through the dimly lit hallway to the back porch. He liked this house. The Thompsons had clearly heated it with wood and space heaters. The electrical wiring and plumbing needed upgrades, and he hoped central heating and air conditioning could be installed. If not, this was still the perfect house to weather a crisis that might force people back to living without the comforts of a stable electrical grid.

As he walked onto the back porch, Brad noticed the large sink that sat against the screen and had a hand pumped faucet. He imagined washing produce from the garden there and getting it ready for canning or freezing. He imagined children playing out here on rainy summer days.

Brad sighed. None of that was going to happen any time soon. They were in the middle of a national crisis, and it would be risky to leave the farm until things felt safer. Meeting a woman under these conditions felt impossible, especially one willing to consider a home this primitive when modern homes with central heat and air were still on the market.

Brad locked the back door and the screen door then drove the golf cart around to the outbuildings. Mr. Thompson had also sold all of his equipment to Brad.

He unlocked the door to a large building with two oversized bays. Inside were a tractor with a cab that was larger than the tractor on Ginny's farm, a large combine, an ATV with a bed, and a riding lawn mower. A small open trailer sat beside a larger one that Brad guessed was about sixteen feet long.

The building had been divided. He walked through the door to the other side and found a woodworking shop. Mr. Thompson had left every piece of machinery a person could want to build things. Brad's first thought was to show this to Mike. The two of them could build just about anything that the group needed.

Everything in the shop was clean and in good condition. Antique hand tools hung on a peg board and filled up shelves. A small portable welder sat in a corner. He didn't know how to use it, but he planned to learn. He assumed that the boxes of rods stacked next to the welder went with the machine.

Brad stepped out of the shop and walked toward the barn. It was sturdy, and the horse stalls were in good condition. Brad doubted this farm had ever been a dairy, although he imagined there had been one or two cows to provide milk to its inhabitants.

The sun was starting to set behind a bank of clouds when Brad decided to return to Ginny's. He had already started thinking of this place as his and the other farm as hers, and that was just fine. That's the way it would be eventually.

Brad parked the golf cart in the equipment shed and plugged it in to recharge. The wind was beginning to blow harder as he approached the house, suggesting a storm was approaching. He saw his three siblings walking toward him.

"You've been gone a long time," Ginny said. "Everything okay?"

"Yes," Brad said with a genuine smile. "I'm fine, but thanks for worrying. I spent the afternoon at the other house. Believe it or not, I bought the place without ever having been through the whole thing. It's pretty cool. It's like stepping back into the late 1800s. It even has an old wood cook stove in the kitchen, a hand pump faucet on the back porch, and a fireplace in every room. I felt at home and at peace there. When things settle down and we don't have to worry about crime, I want to move in. I'd like to plant the garden, but I don't think that's wise this year. Every bit of the food would be stolen before I could get to it, I'm sure. Tom's steer should be proof of that."

Brad looked at Ginny, Mark and Garrett. They were smiling.

"What?" he asked, grabbing his ball cap as the wind blew it from his head.

"Welcome back," Garrett said. "It's good to see the old Brad."

Brad smiled. "It feels good to be back."

Brad opened the back door for his siblings just as rain started to fall. He turned to watch the downpour washing the pollutants from the air. He hoped they would wake up in the morning to a fresh, clean, smoke-free sky.

———◆◇◆———

Switzerland

John Rosen laughed out loud when the news came through that North Korea had attacked South Korea. That was unexpected, but it played right into his hands. Now he just had to stop smiling before his meeting with Mr. Lin.

George let him know that Mr. Lin was waiting in the conference room. John waited exactly five minutes before he walked into the room. Mr. Lin stood until John sat down at the table.

"I thought you had North Korea under control," John said, looking Lin in the eye. He could see anger and distress in Mr. Lin's face.

"Sir," Lin said, "we warned the North Korean dictator to not do that. He acted on his own. Our President is warning their government that we will pull our support if the fighting continues, but at the same time he is warning the rest of the world to stay out of the conflict."

"I hope you can control this, Mr. Lin," John said seriously. "We have discussed other global tasks that were to be accomplished before we allowed North Korea to engage with South Korea. The United States Military in South Korea has become involved out of survival, not intent. We didn't want that, because the United States is still too strong. They will feel obligated to honor their agreement with South Korea to protect that country. Now our timeline is disrupted. You understand, I must hold China responsible for this. Your country promised you could control North Korea."

Mr. Lin clenched his fists, trying hard to control his anger. "Sir, we are getting the situation under control."

John leaned back in his chair and steepled his hands in front of his chest, not breaking eye contact with Lin.

"Mr. Lin," he said, "please let your President know that this may reduce the territory and natural resources available to China. The fighting must stop on the Korean peninsula."

"Yes, Sir," Lin replied.

"Thank you, Mr. Lin. That's all for now." John rose and exited the room, knowing that in his wake, he left an angry Lin who still sat in his chair, looking at the table as though he had been scolded like a schoolboy. John smiled as the door closed behind him. He knew that Lin would report Rosen's disrespect of China to his President.

CHAPTER 18

APRIL 17

North Carolina, USA

Brad opened the office door to get breakfast and jumped back inside. Pete and Bennett ran past him and into the backyard. He heard Bennett's truck start and rush down the driveway. Brad stepped out of the office and looked into the den to see Ginny sitting at the computer, talking on her phone.

"What's going on?" he asked as he walked through the kitchen. He reached the den and sat down beside Ginny, scanning the monitor screens.

"Yeah! What's going on?" Mark asked, walking up behind them. "I looked out the bedroom window to see Bennett's truck rushing out of here like a bat out of hell." He scanned the monitor over Ginny's shoulder. "The cameras aren't showing anything."

"A strange truck pulled into the Johnson's driveway," she said, pointing to the picture that showed the edge of their neighbor's property and their mailbox. Pete and Bennett left to go over there to make sure everything is all right. I called Aaron. He was still asleep, but he woke up quick when I told them what was happening. He said he didn't recognize the truck then hung up. I don't know anything else."

"I'm going over the back way," Mark said and hurried out the back door. Brad heard the four-wheeler start up and race out of the shed.

The cameras allowed Ginny and Brad to see the road between their driveway and the Johnson's property, but they couldn't see what was happening in the Johnson's driveway. Brad got up and opened the front door, propping the screen open so he and Ginny could listen. His heart clenched and he automatically looked to the south when he heard three pops of gunfire echoing across the valley.

"Ginny, that's gunfire," Brad said, hurrying back to the monitors and the unchanged pictures. "Why can't we see anything," he mumbled, running his hands through his hair. "Watch the monitors," he said quickly as he ran out the back of the house, the back door slamming behind him.

Brad ran through the backyard to the campers. He pounded on the doors.

"Get up!" he called.

"What's happening?" Mike asked as his head poked out from his camper door.

Grace and Max asked the same thing from their campers.

"There's gunfire next door," Brad yelled, running back to the house. "Get in the house." Brad ran back into the house and up the stairs. He knocked on the other bedroom doors where adults were sleeping. Alex, Garrett and Robert came out.

"Gunfire at the Johnson's," Brad reported. He continued shouting orders as he ran back down the stairs. "Get up and get everybody downstairs. Robert, you and Leah keep the kids in the basement. Alex, you and Garrett come with me. We need to get weapons."

Within minutes, Brad had sentries at the doors and the upstairs windows. The gunfire had been brief, but they still wouldn't know what had really happened until the other men got back. Everyone remembered the incident from the dreams, but they all knew the dreams could be changed. After what seemed like an eternity, Brad heard the familiar motor of the four-wheeler growing close.

Mark drove into the yard, stopped at the back door and came into the house. He noticed the armed guards.

"Who arranged this?" he asked Max, who was at the back door.

"Brad," Max answered. "As soon as the kid heard gunfire, he woke us all up. The children are downstairs with Leah. Every man has a gun and a post, and you can see Barbara, Erica, and Ceely are fixing breakfast."

"I'm impressed," Mark said.

"So was I," Max replied. "The kid thinks fast on his feet."

"Where is he?" Mark asked.

"He took point at the front door," Max answered, pointing to the front of the house.

"Everyone can stand down," Mark said. "It's over. The Johnson's are fine, but it wasn't pretty."

Mark went to the front door where Brad stood watching the front yard.

"You can stand down. It's over. I'll tell you everything that happened as I know it."

Brad called all clear and everyone gathered in the kitchen. Once Leah fed the children and took them downstairs to get ready for school, the adults made their plates and took seats at the dining room table. No one ate, waiting for Mark to speak. When Leah returned, Mark explained.

"It was already over by the time I got there," he said. "Evidently, two men, late teens according to their drivers' licenses, drove up and demanded that Aaron give them Bonnie. They insisted they knew her, but Bonnie told Carson and Aaron she had no idea who they were. The driver threatened Aaron. When Aaron didn't give them Bonnie, the driver opened fire on Aaron."

Mark paused, letting the information sink in.

"The passenger shot at Pete who was with Bennett in the truck blocking the driveway. Pete killed the passenger. Aaron shot the driver in the chest and Bennett finished him off with a shot through the head. They're disposing of the bodies as we speak."

"Did anyone recognize either of them?" Alex asked.

"I don't remember their names, but they were the same ones from the dream," Mark said. "Carson knew them from high school. The driver was a couple years ahead of Carson and was always acting like a bully. He thinks the passenger was probably a dropout.

Mark exhaled. "Aaron's pretty shaken up. I told him he could move his camper over here for his family and that Carson could take a bunk in the basement with our boys. He's moving Grace, Hannah, Bonnie, and Tina to the camper today, and then he and Donna are moving to the apartment over their barn in the back pasture."

Everyone was quiet, absorbing everything Mark had said.

Mark looked at Ginny. "Are you okay with that? I know it means more people here."

"It's fine," Ginny said, "but I hope that is the one and only episode we have like this. I remember it from the dream, but I hadn't thought it would really happen. I should've known better. Pete and Bennett must have remembered because they were out of here in a flash."

Everyone sat around the table eating their now cold breakfast when Pete and Bennett returned.

"What did you do with the bodies?" Mark asked them quietly

"Aaron put them in the back of their pickup and parked it behind an abandoned farmhouse about two miles down the road," Pete told him. "He hid his anxiety well, but I think he was pretty shaken. They're packing up the girls to move over here today. Carson will bunk with the guys in the basement. Aaron and Donna will move into the barn apartment."

"That's the rest of us, then," Mark said. "We're all here now, just like in the dream."

That afternoon, Brad was in the pasture checking on two of their cows that were supposed to be birthing their calves any day when Aaron brought his camper and his family to the Reed farm. Brad missed the introductions, but everyone else welcomed them.

Heather remembered Grace from the dream and immediately connected with her and Tina about the school. Before the afternoon was over, a curriculum for all ages had been established and the responsibilities of teaching and lesson plans had been shared between them. School would take place every morning for two hours, six days a week. Ginny called Tom Sutton and invited Brady to join them for classes.

Ginny noticed Bonnie and Hannah were at loose ends, uncertain where to fit in. She introduced them to Barbara and Leah who would let them help with meals and food preservation.

Late in the afternoon Brad came back to the house, looking for Ginny.

"One of the cows is having a difficult birth," he told her. "Can you come take a look?"

"Sure," she said. "Which pasture?"

"The lower one between Sutton's and mine," he replied.

"Let me get some supplies," she said. "I'll be right there."

Brad returned to the pasture, and a few minutes later, Ginny drove up in her truck. She got out and looked at the cow.

"Well, the girl is trying to give birth," Ginny said, "but it does seem to be distressing her."

Ginny put on long-armed gloves, reached into the cow and palpated the cervix.

"Oh, this will be easy."

Using both hands, one on the inside and one on the outside of the cow, she rotated the calf and pulled its legs through the cervix and into the birth canal. With another push, the cow added a new member to the herd.

"Poor baby had its leg jammed against the side of the uterus. It may have rotated in time, but it's possible the cow and calf would have both died eventually. Easy fix." Ginny looked closely at the calf. "Ooh. He's a pretty one. Congratulations, Brad, that looks like a future prize-winning bull. I wouldn't make that one into a steer. You need to keep him for breeding. Get some new heifers. Maybe you could get one of Aaron or Tom's cows to mate with it in a couple years. Look at the muscle mass already on the little fellow."

"I see what you mean," Brad said, grinning broadly. "I know some farmers who would love to have that much beef mass in a grown steer. Can you imagine how much money he would bring at the market? Assuming we ever have markets again."

"I know. Sad isn't it," Ginny replied.

Ginny made sure the afterbirth had been delivered intact. When the cow was on her feet and the calf starting to stand, Brad and Ginny returned to the house.

Ginny and Brad walked into the mudroom. Ginny cleaned up in the laundry bathroom, and when she was finished, Brad did the same. By the time he stepped into the kitchen, Ginny was eating and Barbara pulled a foil-wrapped plate from the warmer and handed it to him.

"I heard you have a very nice new bull in your herd," Barbara said.

"I do," Brad grinned. "It's one of the best ones I've seen. I can't wait to see how big he grows. He's going to be huge."

It was dark when Brad finished eating. He was exhausted and just wanted to go to bed. He looked out the back door to see Carson and Bonnie Johnson sitting with the others outside. There was a woman he didn't recognize sitting with them along with two teenage girls he'd never seen before. That must be Donna's sister and her family. Well, he would meet them tomorrow.

Brad didn't even turn on his usual movie. He fell asleep thinking about his new calf.

CHAPTER 19

APRIL 18

North Carolina, USA

Brad woke before dawn. He wasn't surprised. He had fallen asleep early last night. Sighing, he got up, dressed and walked into the kitchen where he settled at the kitchen island with a cup of coffee.

Erica came in and started pulling mixing bowls from the cabinet.

"Please tell me you're making your breakfast burritos," Brad said. His smile widened when she got flour tortillas from the pantry and eggs from the refrigerator.

"I am," Erica said, laughing. "I brought the spices, but Ginny bought cases of them. As long as there are eggs and tortillas, we will have burritos."

Brad's attention shifted to Carson when the teenager came up the stairs and walked straight toward the coffee pot. He poured himself a cup of coffee and sat by Brad.

"Hey Carson," Brad said. "You doing okay?"

Carson nodded as he took a sip of coffee. "I'm good. Missing my own bed, but I'll adjust. I have to say, Brad, I feel a lot safer here than at my house after what happened yesterday."

"I imagine so," Brad said. "We heard what happened."

Carson exhaled hard. "I never want to see a gun pointed at my dad again. I wanted to run out on the porch to help him, but I knew that would have distracted him, and we would have both been shot. Plus, it took everything I had to keep Mom and Bonnie calm."

"That was wise, Carson," Brad said, taking a sip of his coffee. "How's Bonnie adjusting?"

"Man, I feel bad for her," Carson said, shaking his head. "She cried all day yesterday and kept promising she didn't know those guys. I believe her. She jumps at her own shadow now. I know it will get better, but I still worry about her."

"Have you and your dad got everything caught up on your farm?" Brad asked, intentionally changing the subject. He caught Erica giving him an approving smile as she shaped the burritos.

"Yeah," Carson replied. "Corn's in the ground. We planted grass in the garden plot because it's so close to the road, but we left about an acre in the back of one field open. We're going to plant the garden there this year."

"Smart," Brad said. "I increased our garden, too, but ours can't be seen from the road."

Grace, Bonnie, Hannah and Tina came inside through the back door and immediately went to speak to Erica.

"Is that your aunt?" Brad asked Carson quietly.

"Yeah. That's Aunt Grace. Tina's with her, and Hannah is walking with Bonnie."

Brad noticed Bonnie was holding onto Hannah.

"I hope Bonnie can get to where she feels safe here," Brad said.

Erica turned and handed Brad and Carson each a plate with two breakfast burritos.

"Amazing," Brad said, grinning at his plate. He felt his stomach growling as he inhaled the aroma of eggs and spices. "Thanks, Erica.

You're a champ."

"Don't you forget it," Erica said with a smile before turning back to wrap more burritos.

Grace started to walk past the island when Carson said, "Aunt Grace, this is Brad Reed. You didn't get to meet him yesterday. He was out on the farm."

"Hello, Brad," Grace said, extending her hand in greeting. "It's nice to meet you."

"Nice to meet you, too," Brad replied, wiping his fingers on a napkin before shaking her hand. "Welcome to the farm. I heard you had a hard trip up from Charlotte."

Grace rolled her eyes. "I don't ever want to repeat that experience, but I would do it again to be here and safe." She gestured to the girls. "You already know Bonnie. This is Hannah and that's Tina."

"Welcome to the farm," Brad said. He looked at Bonnie.

"I heard you were pretty brave yesterday. I'm glad you're here."

Bonnie smiled. "Thanks, Brad. I'm glad I'm here now, too."

Erica came over and told the group they could get burritos. Brad and Carson finished theirs without waiting for the rest of the group to get their breakfast. When they were finished, they rinsed their plates and went outside to start working.

Tina watched Brad pass. She stared at him. This was not the farm in her dream, but that man was. So far, he was the only familiar part of the dream she had seen. She didn't know what that meant, but she would be patient until it was revealed.

Halfway to the barn, Carson's phone buzzed in his pocket. He pulled it out and froze.

"What is it?" Brad asked.

Carson turned the phone toward him.

"Look at this," Carson said, pointing to the screen. "This truck keeps driving back and forth in front of our house. Look, it's coming back now. It's probably in front of yours."

"We'd better go back inside and see if we're needed," Brad said. "Does your dad have access to this footage, too?"

"Yeah, he does," Carson said. He looked up to see the golf cart coming toward them from the pasture. "He must have seen it. He and Mom are on the way."

When they reached Brad and Carson, Aaron got out of the cart. "Did you see it, Carson?"

"Yeah," Carson said. "We were just about to go back inside to see what happened."

Aaron, Carson, Donna and Brad entered the house and headed for the monitors where Pete, Ginny, Mark and Bennett stood discussing the truck.

Mark looked up. "Hey Aaron. Figured you might be getting here pretty fast. That truck came back past our place and kept going. I called Tom. He saw it, too. It passed his place heading out and hasn't come back."

Brad looked around. Donna was sitting at the table with Bonnie, distracting her from this conversation.

"That decides it for us," Mark said. "Our mailbox comes up today, and we make the drive impassable. Aaron, what do you want to do about your drive and yard?"

Mike, listening from the dining room table, joined in. After a long discussion, they settled on a plan.

Brad slipped out the back door and got the tractor. Instead of heading to the fields as planned, he drove to the end of the driveway, removed the mailbox, then plowed and disced the earth about twenty yards into the woods. The driveway would be well hidden from the road. Once the earth was prepared, Brad returned the tractor to the equipment shed and used the ATV to carry grass seed out to the road. He spread the seed across the area and said a silent prayer for more rain.

When Brad returned to the house, everyone not helping with food preparation, including the teenage boys, was hammering nails through the planks they planned to bury. He joined them. They planted rebar spikes where the grass seed had been sown, leaving the metal high enough to stop vehicles from entering the property but low enough to disappear once the grass grew in.

They buried the nail-studded planks along Aaron's drive and yard, then nailed sheets of plywood over the windows and doors. By mid morning, they moved to Brad's yard and repeated the process, burying the planks with the nails facing up along his drive and yard.

As Garrett worked, he watched the others and marveled at how this mix of friends and strangers had secured all three homes so quickly. Their ability to work together pleased him, and he wondered what the future held, hoping this camaraderie would last.

It was an unseasonably warm day for mid April, and by the time they finished, everyone came back to the house hot and tired. Brad dropped into a chair under the large oak trees in the backyard, their leaves still small and pale. He drank a cold can of soda, then leaned back and held the chilled aluminum across his forehead. The cold felt good.

From the back porch, Leah called that lunch was ready. Brad stayed where he was, too worn out to fight the crowd of hungry people that funneled through the door that Leah had just gone inside.

Brad watched the kids carry their plates to the picnic tables that were scattered in the backyard. Carson, Bonnie, Hannah, Tina, Adam, Michael, and Brett crowded around one table. The younger kids gathered at another. Brad got up and went into the house.

He didn't notice Tina's eyes follow him.

After lunch Brad went to the pasture to check on the new calf and its mother, both of which were doing well. Afterward he rode to his place and began to look through the rest of the buildings. He found rolls of six-foot-tall game fencing and the fence posts.

He had enough fencing stored at Ginny's to protect her front and back yards, the garden, the campers and the equipment shed. He could use what he found in his buildings to put around his house and the large building with the bays. Brad smiled when he opened a plastic storage bin to find the U-shaped clips that pinned the fencing to the posts; leaning against the wall was a wire stretcher. Maybe he could get Garrett or Mike to help him.

Brad rode back to Ginny's with plans whirling in his mind. He would put the fencing around his house. Then, it would be time to plant a garden of his own. Brad thought about driving to town to buy some starter plants but remembered the farm and garden store was probably closed. He had seeds. He could get Michael to help him sow those in a flat tonight.

After dinner Brad took Michael out to the barn. Michael helped him spread potting soil into two large flats. He showed him how to spread the seeds and gently pour a little soil on top, then let Michael sow the second flat on his own.

They carried the flats to the laundry room and placed them on the table next to the washing machine where Ginny usually folded laundry. Brad pulled grow lights from a storage cabinet, placed them over the flats, and turned them on. Michael watched the whole setup with intense concentration.

"That's all of it, Michael," Brad said. "Only thing left is watering them."

Brad took a small watering can from a shelf, filled it with water and poured a gentle shower over one flat. He handed the can to Michael and watched him water the other flat.

"Normally I'd leave this set up in the barn, but these aren't normal times," Brad said. "This room has no window. No light will shine through in the middle of the night like it would down at the barn.

A light at night is like a beacon saying, 'come to me!' We don't want anyone stealing our plants. The stores are almost empty, so food is like gold now. We need to protect it."

Michael nodded in understanding.

Tina had just hurried up the stairs from the basement. She walked toward the back door on her way to her camper, but the laundry room door suddenly opened. Without time to stop, Tina slammed into someone and bounced back like she had hit a wall. She started to fall backward, but two strong hands grabbed her arms and held her steady. She looked up and saw that it was Brad.

"I'm sorry," she said. "I didn't see you."

"I'm sorry, too," Brad said, chuckling. "I'm not used to having to watch the traffic when I come out of a room." He looked at her. "You're Tina, right?"

"Yes," Tina smiled. "You're Brad?"

"Yes," he said, nodding. "Are you settling in all right? I know you were with your family at the Johnson's and now you've been uprooted to another place."

Tina looked confused. "Yes, I was at the Johnson's, but they aren't my family."

Brad raised his eyebrows in confusion and looked down at her.

"I thought you came from Charlotte with Grace," he said.

"I did," Tina said, "but we were neighbors. We aren't related."

"If you were neighbors, why didn't your parents come with you?" Brad asked, frowning and crossing his arms.

"I didn't live with my parents. They're in Virginia," Tina answered.

"Okay," Brad said, blinking and shaking his head. "I am really confused. Why are you living on your own in a place like Charlotte, and why did your parents allow it."

Tina suddenly realized what was happening. He had mistaken her for one of the teenagers. She almost laughed.

"I teach at the same school Grace does. I'm a high school math teacher." Tina grinned and waited for his reaction.

"What?" Brad asked incredulously, droping his arms and leaning his head forward in shock. "You're a teacher? I thought you were Bonnie's age."

Tina laughed. He liked her laugh. It was light and almost melodic.

"Most people think I'm younger than I am," she said. "I'm only five feet four, and I have a baby face."

Brad leaned back against the doorframe and crossed his arms again. He looked down at her petite frame.

"You really don't look old enough to be teaching," Brad said. "I bet that has its advantages and disadvantages."

"It does," she said. "When I was in college, I could never go anywhere with my friends without having to show my ID. But, by the same token, I have friends who are already frantically looking at anti-aging products." She shrugged. "It's a tradeoff."

"I would like to hear your story about how you wound up here on this farm," Brad said, "but it's late, and I assume you were heading to your camper."

Tina smiled, "I was. I'll see you tomorrow."

"Yeah," Brad said. "I'll see you tomorrow."

He watched her walk out the door and across the yard. A teacher. He would never have guessed that. Brad straightened and went into the office. He was tired. He climbed into bed, but for some reason he could not stop thinking about the young-looking math teacher.

———◇———

Washington DC

President Douglas Massey listened as the Chairman of the Federal

Reserve, the Secretary of Defense, and the Director of the Office of Management and Budget delivered their reports. The stock market had lost over sixty percent of its value. The dollar had collapsed worldwide, and inflation was rising so fast that hyperinflation was expected within a few weeks. No countries were buying U.S. Treasuries anymore. The government could no longer meet its financial obligations; the nation was in an economic free fall. If they were going to have any chance of surviving this, drastic measures would be required.

Donald Evans, Secretary of Defense, reported that he was recalling troops from around the world back to the United States. They could no longer afford the foreign bases. The dollar was simply too weak.

Massey decided to temporarily withhold money from government programs and suspend social security checks for May. In another few days, the banks would close. If he played this correctly, he could position himself as the country's savior. When desperation peaked, he could authorize bailout checks to the citizens and reopen the banks.

When the meeting ended and the office emptied, Massey smiled. This could work, but first he needed to take care of some urgent matters. Massey called his family members and closest friends, swore them to secrecy, and told them to pull their money out of the banks.

⸺◇⸺

Switzerland

John Rosen smiled as he watched the news. The United States was in a complete economic collapse, and U.S. troops were being recalled. Soon, the world would be his.

CHAPTER 20

APRIL 19

North Carolina, USA

Garrett, Robert, Mike and Alex helped Brad sink the fence posts and stretch the game fence around his house and the large shop. Brad felt better about the security of his new home.

It was day ten of the crisis. At Ginny's house, everyone had fallen into a predictable routine.

The television stayed on so they wouldn't miss any news. Food and supplies were carefully monitored and utilized. The outhouse and outdoor shower were finished, and everyone worked in the gardens to plant, pull weeds, and harvest what was ripe.

Looking around at the people going about their chores and activities, Ginny was glad things were flowing well, but she couldn't escape the nagging thought they were getting too complacent.

Washington, DC

Donald Evans could see that President Douglas Massey was angry. Jacob Miller had not reported to work in days, and no one could find him. It seemed the man had disappeared. Massey had relied so heavily on Miller that he felt alone and adrift without him.

Donald had a good idea what had happened to Miller. Either the people who had benefitted from Miller's treason had killed him to cover their tracks, or Miller had fled the country before that could happen. Unfortunately, Donald knew that he and the rest of the Cabinet would be left to clean up the mess Miller created.

Switzerland

John Rosen leaned against the railing on the chalet's balcony, staring at the Alps and planning his next moves when he heard George Thomas open the sliding glass doors and step outside.

"John," George said.

"Yes?" Rosen asked, turning toward his friend.

"It seems we can't find Jacob Miller or Greg Becker," George said. "They're not answering any of their devices. They have disappeared."

"How could that happen?" Rosen asked.

"Evidently Miller is quite an expert at covering his tracks," George answered. "He ditched his phones. Computer, too. My guess is that he assumed he has outlived his usefulness with us and fled the country. Do you want me to expand the search?"

Rosen stood thoughtfully for a moment.

"No," he said. "His wife and daughter are in Belize. That's where Miller is heading. Let's use our manpower more efficiently for the moment, but we won't forget about Mr. Miller. Leaving him alone will make him lower his guard. Then, if he gets in the way or decides to tell what he knows, we can act."

George nodded and went back into the house. John followed him, and they went to the locked study in the chalet to work until their evening meeting with The Committee.

CHAPTER 21

APRIL 20

North Carolina, USA

At breakfast, Ginny's phone rang. After a brief conversation, a picture notification popped up.

"Brad," she said, holding the phone where he could see it. "Recognize anyone?"

"That's Dwight Hall on the right," Brad said, setting down his coffee mug to lean closer. "I don't know the one on the left."

"These pictures came from Tom," Ginny said, pulling her phone back. "His cameras caught them sneaking into his pasture again last night. According to the time stamp they were only in there for about fifteen minutes before leaving. You can see they left empty-handed." She shook her head. "Just like the dream."

"Could the sheriff be in on it?" Max asked.

"I hope not," Brad replied. "He's always been an honest guy who's worked hard. Dwight, on the other hand, is lazy and has a history of taking the easy way out, even when we were kids. He's going to sneak onto the wrong person's land and get himself shot. He's got a wife and kids. I wonder how they're doing through all this."

Garrett had been listening. He called Brett over and whispered. Brett disappeared downstairs and returned a moment later holding what looked like a miniature satellite dish.

Garrett cleared his throat for everyone's attention.

"I think it's time to bring out the electronic ace card," he said, patting Brett's shoulder. "If they can't find cows near the road, they might use drones. They did in the dream. We have a radar system that can pick up drones as far away as two miles. If they're coming this way, that gives us time to get into place and shoot them from the sky before they reach our pastures."

"Good call, Garrett!" Mark said, smiling. "Brett, can you keep it going and monitor it?"

"Sure," Brett said. "I can set it up for continuous monitoring. It will alert my phone if it detects anything."

"Where do you want to put it?" Mark asked.

"Dad and I think the top of the barn, near the hayloft, will work," Brett replied. "It'll clamp onto the edge of the roof and be easy to remove if we need to take it down."

Garrett and Brett gathered the radar system and tools and started toward the barn. As they walked, Garrett thought about how different their responses were compared to the dream. In the dream they'd only been able to react with whatever they had on hand. Now they had a chance to be proactive, to set up defenses before they were even needed.

Tina watched everything from her place at the breakfast table. Her eyes flickered up when she heard Ginny and Garrett mention something about a dream. She wondered what kind of dream they had and if it had been anything like hers. Just knowing someone else may have had the same experience was reassuring. She made a mental note to ask them about it once things settled down.

Once the others left to start their projects for the day, Mark and Ginny moved to the den and turned on the morning news. Brad and Alex walked over to watch with them.

"What are they saying?" Alex asked.

"Well," Mark said, "first the government is not going to put any more money into assistance programs. Social security checks will be withheld in May. They're diverting all funds to the military. I think the government is broke."

"And second?" Ginny asked.

"China has announced it's now North Korea's ally," Mark continued. "They stopped the fighting between North and South Korea, but they've warned that any country who fires more missiles into the North will face the full force of the Chinese army. Russia has completely taken over Ukraine. They're invading Georgia so they can get to Armenia and 'protect it' from Azerbaijan. They also have troops on the Ukrainian border with Poland. NATO is complaining to the United Nations about Russia while moving forces into Poland."

Ginny looked at Brad. "Better make the garden bigger."

Brad looked at the clock and turned to Mark and Ginny.

"We did it!" he exclaimed.

"What did we do?" Ginny asked.

"At this time in the dream you were working on Daniel Speaks after he'd been shot. He's not here. We changed the dream!"

Ginny looked up at the clock. "Oh my gosh. You're right!" Ginny laughed with abandon and hugged Brad. "We did it. We changed things and no one was hurt."

She looked at Brad and Mark. "Maybe this is one of the things we're supposed to do, keep Daniel Speaks and Hank Miller safe."

Brad was glad Ginny was happy. He didn't want to burst her bubble by reminding her they only knew the future up to the arrival of the motorcycle gang.

Garrett and Brett had just placed the radar on the barn. On their way back to the house, Brett received an alert on his phone. Garrett grabbed the two-way radio to alert the security desk.

"Yeah, Garrett," Mark said into the radio. "What is it?"

"Mark, we just put the radar system up, and it's already picked up a drone coming from the north."

"Can you see it?" Mark asked.

"I don't see anything yet, but I don't have any binoculars. According to the readout, it should be crossing Tom Sutton's farm about now."

"I can see it," Garrett said after a moment. He paused. "What?"

"What do you mean?" Mark asked. "What happened?"

"It disappeared," Garrett answered.

Mark grinned, then said into the radio, "That would have been Bennett shooting it out of the sky."

By midmorning, Brad walked out the back door and saw Brady Sutton climbing off his four-wheeler near the barn.

"Brady?" Brad asked, surprised. "Is everything alright?"

"Yes, Sir," Brady answered. "My dad sent me over for school."

Brad nodded in understanding. "Come with me."

Brad led Brady inside and down the stairs, where he introduced him to Grace, Tina and Heather. Brad looked around, surprised at how much everything had changed. Portable tables were in place, dividing the room into elementary, middle, and high school sections. He watched Tina settle Brady into a chair next to the other teenagers and explain his work. Brad turned and went back upstairs. The kid was in good hands.

Brad went to the equipment shed. He started the tractor and backed out. He was going to expand the garden yet again. He knew what Ginny wanted. She wanted a surplus.

CHAPTER 22

APRIL 21

North Carolina, USA

The buzz of a news alert woke Brad. He got up in the dim, early-morning light, dressed and went to the den to turn on the television. Bennett sat at the computer desk, his eyes fixed on the monitors.

"Morning, Bennett," Brad said.

"Morning." Bennett didn't look away from the screen.

"I got a news alert about the banks. Mind if I turn on the television?"

"No, go ahead," Bennett replied. "I'd like to hear it, too."

Ginny came down the stairs, yawning as she pulled her hair into a ponytail.

"I got a news alert," she said, heading toward the television. "What's going on?"

"I'm about to find out," Brad said, turning the television to the Winston-Salem station.

"What does it say?" Bennett asked.

"Russia has claimed all the land in Eastern Europe, saying their Russian-speaking citizens want to be a part of Russia. They've conquered most of Georgia and are on their way to Armenia. NATO is blustering, and the U.S. is staying quiet. Iran, Iraq, and Turkey have allied against Israel. China has attacked Taiwan. Japan is still complaining to the UN about the island dispute with China.

"And the last report says the President and the Federal Reserve have declared a bank holiday. Every bank in the U.S. is closed today. Too many people must have tried to pull their money out at once. And there you have it, for now."

"No one has to invade us," Bennett said. "We are imploding from within." Bennett paused, then stiffened. "Brad, come take a look at this."

Brad leaned over Bennett's shoulder. The screen showed Brad's house. In the early-morning sunlight, a truck pulled to the edge of the road. Two men got out of the truck and stood staring at the house.

"I'm going over there," Brad said, turning toward the back door.

"Not without me," Bennett said.

"Or me," Pete said, coming into the den.

"I'll watch the monitors," Ginny said, moving toward the computer.

"I'm taking the four-wheeler in the back way," Brad said to Bennett and Pete as he tugged on his boots in the mudroom. "Give me a minute, then take a truck and come up behind them."

"I'll take the golf cart and come in quietly from the north," Mark said, following Brad out. "We will have them on three sides."

"Thanks," Brad said, tossing Mark the key to the new fence before sprinting to the equipment shed.

A few minutes later, Ginny saw Brad on the camera feed, driving the four-wheeler around the corner of his house.

Brad stopped the four-wheeler just short of the nails that had been buried to stop trespassers. The men watched him.

"Can I help you?" Brad asked. "I'm Brad Reed. You're on my

property."

"I'm Jack Bost," the younger of the two men said. "This is Rob Smith, my brother-in-law. We're staying with our families in his parents' home on the other side of the clinic."

"I know," Brad said calmly.

Jack looked surprised. "How do you know?"

"These are uncertain times," Brad said. "We keep track of things for our safety. What do you want with my property?"

"We thought the Thompsons lived here," Jack said.

"They did," Brad replied. "I bought it from them."

"Yeah?" Jack asked, his tone turning sharp. "Can you prove it, or did you just decide to take it because they were gone?"

Brad rolled his eyes but kept his temper in check.

"I can prove it," he said. "The deed's registered with the county. Go check it."

"That's convenient," Jack scoffed. "They're closed."

"Sorry," Brad said with a shrug. "But I do own it."

"We need the space," Jack said. "We're running out of room back at the house. We were hoping to split up and part of us move in here."

"I'm sorry," Brad said, "but I can't allow that. We're crowded at the Reed farm too. I'm planning to move some of our people here."

"Right," Jack said. "You're moving people into a place with boarded windows and a fence around it."

"Yes, I am," Brad said. "The fence and plywood are there because the house is too close to the road not to secure it. Look, I'm sorry you're running out of space, but this isn't an option for you. You'll need to look elsewhere."

"But this is the closest place," Jack argued. "And it's empty."

"How do you know?" Brad asked. "Have you been inside?"

Jack hesitated. "Uh... no, but you can tell."

Brad sighed and called out, "Mark. Come out of the house."

Mark stepped out from behind house, inside of the fence. He carried a shotgun.

"Having trouble, Brad?" Mark asked.

Jack and Rob froze.

"See, I told you. I'm using it," Brad said firmly. He paused. "It's almost summer. You've got time to plant a garden and even add a room onto your place if you need to. Do what you have to do to make surviving comfortable, because that's what this is now. Surviving."

"What happened to the Johnsons?" Rob asked. "Their house is all boarded up, and no one's there. We could use that house."

"I wouldn't," Brad replied. "There's already been one gunfight there and people were killed. It's too close to the road to be safe. At least your place sits back from the highway."

"Come on, Jack," Rob said, tugging his arm. "Neither house will work. Let's go before someone gets mad or crazy."

"Sorry," Rob said, looking at Brad. "We're leaving."

The two men turned to go to their truck and stopped. Pete and Bennett were leaning against Bennett's truck, watching them, each with a shotgun resting across his arm.

Rob looked around. Three armed men were watching them. Brad was the only without a gun in his hand, and Rob was sure one was nearby. From the casual way they held their weapons, these men has seen at least one gunfight.

"Rob," Brad said.

Rob stopped and looked back.

"There's always someone around," Brad said. "If you need anything or need to talk with Aaron Johnson, leave a note on the fence. I'll find it as long as you don't leave it in the rain."

Rob nodded in understanding.

"Thanks," he said, climbing into his truck.

"Why'd you give in like that?" Jack asked with disgust once they were back in Rob's truck. "I'd bet money that other guy doesn't live there. He probably came in on another ATV. We could move in.

They'll never know."

"Shut up, Jack," Rob said impatiently. "Do you ever listen to your-self? You could have gotten us killed back there. Three armed men watched two of us, and they've already been in at least one gunfight. The bad guys must have lost because Aaron Johnson is still around somewhere. Think for once. Brad Reed offered us an olive branch. We'd better take it."

Rob pulled a piece of paper and a pen from his glove compartment and started writing a note.

"What are you doing?" Jack asked.

"Getting help," Rob said. "If I don't, we're going to die."

Rob got out, clipped the note to the fence, then climbed back into his truck and headed home.

Pete and Bennett were still watching when Rob drove by. Rob gave them a quick salute and continued on.

"That one has sense," Pete said. "Proper salute, too. Which branch do you think?"

"Maybe one day we'll ask," Bennett said as he retrieved the note.

Back at Ginny's house, Bennett handed Brad the note from Rob. Brad read it.

"Rob says he brought seeds, but there's no large equipment left on the farm to plow a garden. He's asked for help." He paused. "Well, that's a good start. Hopefully he can keep his hotheaded broth-er-in-law under control."

"We think Rob has been in the military," Bennett murmured to Mark. "That salute was correct, not the sloppy kind people fake."

Mark raised an eyebrow. "Maybe we should find out. Let's pay him a visit after lunch.

Brad grabbed a cold soda and dropped in a chair in the den.

"You all right?" Ginny asked from the computer.

Brad nodded and took a long drink.

"That was stressful," he said. "I'm not trained in chicken the way Mark, Pete, and Bennett are. They were cool as cucumbers. I was trembling in my boots."

"Didn't look that way on the camera," Ginny said. "You looked like you were handling yourself well."

"Thanks, Ginny," Brad said, grinning. "My ego needed that."

"You're welcome," Ginny said, laughing. "That's what sisters are for, ego soothing."

Tina was getting ready to go to the basement to help with the school that started at ten. She watched the easy banter between Brad and Ginny, and it made her miss her own family. Tears welled in her eyes, and she slipped out the back door before anyone could see her. The high school kids were working on English; they wouldn't miss her for a while. She could hide out in the camper.

Before she reached the camper, Tina saw Grace slip inside. She stopped short, suddenly unsure where to go. Tina wiped her eyes. The farm was huge, yet she couldn't find a private corner. She drifted toward the barn, and to her surprise, it was empty. She slipped to the far side of the building, crouched against the wall, and finally let the grief spill out.

Brad drained the last swig of his soda and stood up. "I have work to do. See you at lunch, Ginny."

"See ya," she answered.

Brad headed to the barn. He was just about to step inside when he heard someone crying. He rounded the corner and saw Tina sitting on the ground, knees pulled to her chest, and her head buried in the nest of her arms. Her shoulders shook. Brad walked toward her, careful not to startle her, but knowing he couldn't just walk away.

"Tina?" he asked quietly.

Tina's head snapped up. Her cheeks flushed, and she looked away, swiping at her eyes with her shirtsleeves.

"Yes?"

"Are you all right? What's wrong?" he asked.

"I'm fine," Tina sniffled. "Just... homesick. It's hard not knowing how your family is."

Brad sat beside her on the ground. "Where's your family?"

"Rural Virginia, southeast of Roanoke," she answered.

"That's tough," Brad said. "I know you worry about them. I bet they worry about you, too."

"The last time I talked to them was the day we got to Aaron and Donna's," she said. "I told them I was safe, told them not to worry... but I haven't been able to reach them since."

"Let me see your phone," Brad said, holding out his hand.

Tina handed it to him.

"Look," he said, pointing at the screen, "you have no service." He pulled out his phone. "See, I have full bars. It's the carrier. Ours is local, so it works better out here."

Brad put his number in her phone's contacts and gave it back to Tina.

Then he handed her his own phone. "Call your family."

He pointed to his number on her phone. "Tell them to call that number. If I'm not nearby, or I'm on the tractor, they can leave a message. You can use my phone any time as long as the service holds."

Tina took his phone and dialed her home. Brad stood and walked away to give her privacy. He'd barely taken a few steps when he heard her whisper, "Mama?" and break into tears. He hoped they were happy tears.

Thirty minutes later Tina found him removing the plow on the tractor. He needed to smooth the ground he had just plowed to expand the garden. She handed him the phone.

"Thank you so much. It was good to hear them. They're all doing well, and they're relieved that I've found a safe place."

"I'm glad you connected with them," Brad said, smiling. "Anytime you get homesick, you come get me and I will hand you the phone. Anytime, Tina. Remember that."

Tina impulsively hugged Brad.

"Thank you, Brad," she said. "This is the nicest thing anyone has done for me since I moved to Huntersville. Well... except for Grace bringing me with her. I will never stop being grateful for that. I don't think I could have survived all this in that apartment."

Surprised, Brad hugged her back. He liked the way she felt in his arms. When Tina let go, she was smiling.

"I need to get back," she said. "They're probably wondering where the math teacher is."

"I'll walk you back," Brad said, following her out of the barn. "Tell me about your family."

On the way to the house, Tina told him about her parents, her brother, her sister, and their families. She was the youngest. When Brad left her at the back door, Tina was like a different person. She was smiling more than she had since she arrived. Brad thought she was pretty when she smiled.

During lunch Brad talked with Mark and Garrett.

"I'm taking the tractor to the Smith farm this afternoon," Brad said between bites of his sandwich. "Rob Smith has asked for help. I feel it's important to extend the hand of friendship as soon as possible considering the confrontation we had this morning."

"I agree," Mark said. "Pete, Max, Bennett and I are going with you, but not because we think it's dangerous to go. Rob Smith did something this morning that we think says military. We want to get to know him and see if he has served."

"Okay," Brad said. "Go on ahead. You can tell him I'm coming. Help him pick out a good spot away from the road for me to plow and get the ground ready for his garden."

After lunch, Mark drove to the Smith house. Pete, Bennett, Alex, and Max rode along. He pulled into the driveway and parked behind the vehicles already there. The men got out of the truck. Mark walked forward while the others stood behind the truck.

Rob and Jack came out onto the porch. Rob was unarmed, but Jack carried a shotgun.

"Rob," Mark said, keeping his hands visible, "we're unarmed and mean no harm. Can you ask your brother-in-law to get rid of the firearm?"

Rob exhaled sharply, irritated. "Jack, take that back inside."

Jack didn't move.

"Jack," Rob repeated, voice firm. "I said take the shotgun back inside."

Jack gave a petty snort and went back into the house.

Rob approached the truck and extended his hand. "Mark. It's good to see you under better circumstances. What can I do for you?"

Before Mark could answer, Max called out from behind the truck. "Major Smith!"

Rob's face lit with recognition. "Lieutenant Benton! What a small world."

Max came around the truck. The two men gave each other a full arm grip and a brief, solid hug.

Max turned to the others. "Guys, this is Major Robert Smith, my CO on deployment. Major, this is Pete Flinn, Army; Alex Freeman, Army; and Bennett Grimes, Marines. You already know Mark, Army as well. Also, Sharon Ingram, our medic, is back at the farmhouse."

Each man shook Rob's hand.

"We had the impression you'd served," Mark said. "We thought we'd come over and get to know you."

The group turned toward the back of the house when they heard the low rumble of Brad's tractor.

Rob tensed until Mark said, "That's Brad. He's on the tractor and going to make a garden plot for you. Where do you want it? He suggested somewhere out of sight from the road."

"There's an old plot behind the barn," Rob said. "It can't be seen from the road."

Rob walked over to meet Brad, who had stopped the tractor and climbed down. They spoke briefly. Brad nodded, then climbed back into the cab, restarted the tractor and drove behind the barn. A few minutes later, the sound shifted as the plow began turning the earth.

"I really appreciate this," Rob said. "Dad sold his large equipment. There are a few hand tools left, but nothing that could break the ground easily. Everything hit so fast; it really caught me off guard. As soon as the President declared a state of emergency, I sent Sarah, my wife, to the grocery store, and I went to the farm and garden store for seeds. It's been a while, but I'm hoping the muscle memory of gardening will come back."

"I'm sure it will," Mark replied. "Do you need anything else?"

"Information," Rob said. "What happened at the Johnson farm?"

Mark turned to Pete. "You were there. You tell it."

Pete relayed the story about the men in the truck who came for Aaron's teenage daughter. No one knew how they learned about her.

Rob's face darkened. "I don't like the sound of that. I have a ten-year-old son and a fourteen-year-old daughter. Marley's girl is eight. What you described worries me."

"I get it," Mark said. "I have a five-year-old daughter and a ten-year-old son. We have three teachers at the farm. The kids have classes every morning. Tom Sutton's fourteen-year-old son comes over. You're welcome to send your kids."

"Thanks," Rob said. "I would like that. The lack of education has worried me."

Footsteps sounded on the porch. The group turned to see the rest of the Smith family. Rob motioned for them to come down into the yard. A woman who looked to be in her forties approached. She was dressed in designer jeans, a soft blouse, and sandals with two-inch heels.

"This is Sarah, my wife," Rob said then pointed to the teenage girl. "That's my daughter, Amanda, and behind her is my son, Robbie."

Another woman came out of the house. She was dressed in jeans, a t-shirt, and comfortable athletic shoes.

"This is Marley, my sister," Rob said.

"Marley Smith," Mark said, "I remember you. I was a couple years ahead of you in school, but we rode the same school bus."

"Mark Reed," Marley said. "Of course I remember. How are you?" Marley gestured to the little girl holding her hand. "This is my daughter, Abby. I heard you met my husband, Jack, this morning."

Jack had reappeared on the porch, arms crossed, staring down at the men. He gave a curt nod, more out of obligation than greeting.

The group heard the tractor engine shift, and the rumble faded away. They recognized that Brad had finished plowing and was headed back to the farm. Marley and Rob continued talking with the men from the Reed farm.

Bennett's attention drifted. He noticed that Sarah Smith looked bored, almost irritated. Jack's posure was all false bravado, chest out and chin up, but his eyes were dull with disinterest. Bennett thought this family was already cracking at the seams.

A few minutes later, Brad returned with a different attachment on the tractor. He smoothed the ground and readied it for planting. When he was done, he parked near the group and climbed out of the cab.

He walked straight to Rob. "I plowed and disced an acre for you. It's ready for you to lay off the rows and plant. It's a perfect time for planting. I have some tomato plants started back at the house. They're small yet, but I'll bring you some when they get bigger. I'll have quite a few with plenty to share."

Rob shook Brad's hand. "I really appreciate this, Brad. What do I owe you for your time and fuel?"

"Let's just be friends and neighbors," Brad said, smiling. "That's all I want."

Rob returned the smiled. "Done. I'd like that, too."

"We should get back," Mark said, "and I guess you need to start a garden." He handed Rob a piece of paper. "My cell number. Call if you need anything or run into trouble."

Max also gave Rob his cell phone number. Rob exchanged his own number.

Mark paused before getting into his truck. "One more thing. "Don't try to drive up our driveway. We plowed it, seeded it with grass, and left sharp rebar sticking up to stop anything with tires."

Rob looked at Mark with a raised eyebrow.

"That's a result of the trouble at the Johnson's," Mark said, giving Rob a knowing look. "Brad's driveway is spiked too. I'm glad you didn't try to drive in there this morning."

"Understood," Rob said. "So am I."

Mark, Pete, Alex, Max and Bennett turned and got back in the truck.

"They're in big trouble," Bennett said when the doors were closed.

"What makes you say that?" Mark asked as he started the engine.

"First, Jack is worthless, has a temper, and is probably lazy," Bennett said. "Secondly, Sarah, Rob's wife, is soft and spoiled. She won't last long. I wouldn't be surprised if she and Jack take one of the cars and leave under the cover of darkness looking for greener pastures in town. Neither one wants to be here, but neither one of them has a clue about what's happening or what it will take to survive. They're still living in the America they remember. They won't adapt."

"You got all that from one meeting?" Mark asked.

"I'm observant," was all Bennett said.

Brad showered, changed his clothes and came out of the bathroom just as Leah announced dinner. As usual he was last in line. When he got his plate, the only open seat at the table was beside Tina.

He smiled as he put his plate down and sat beside her.

"Hey," he said. "I hope you're feeling better than you were this morning."

"Yes, thanks to you," Tina said, giving him a bright smile. "You have no idea how much that meant to me."

She put her hand on his arm. "Thank you so much."

It was a small, unconscious gesture, but it hit Brad harder than expected. It had only been a few weeks since his breakup with Holly, but it felt like years with everything that had happened since. The warmth from Tina's hand felt natural on his skin and held the promise of friendship. He wondered if there could be more.

Chapter 23

April 22

North Carolina, USA

Breakfast was over, and Brad was sipping a leisurely second cup of coffee when Brett suddenly came running up the stairs.

"Drone!" he shouted. "There's a drone coming!" He ran out the back door, and the adults followed closely behind him.

"Oh, no," Mark said, squinting against the brightness of the morning sun. "I hear it. It's getting close."

"There it is," Adam shouted, pointing north.

They could see the drone flying in a zig zag pattern over Tom Sutton's farm.

"It's looking for the cows," Garrett said.

While they were watching, it disappeared in a puff of black smoke with fagments of metal flying across the sky. The group watched the pieces fall to earth, scattering across their pastures. Brad looked aross the yard at the barn loft. Through the loft's opening, he could see Bennett moving toward the ladder.

Bennett emerged from the barn, walking across the back yard. When he got close enough, Mark called, "Did it get close enough to see our cows?"

"Yep," Bennett replied as he walked up to the group. "I could see through the scope that it was right over the northern most part of the pasture, and there were cows directly under it."

Brad balled his fist and let out a rarely used expletive.

"I'm going to be spending the night in that pasture," he said emphatically. "I will not sit by and let someone butcher my cows."

"I'll go with you," Bennet said.

"Me, too," replied Pete and Alex together.

"Okay," Mark said. "Max, Sharon and I will stay here as backup."

Brad was angry. His pulse bounded, and he took deep breaths trying to calm down. He turned and jumped on the four-wheeler. The engine roared to life, and he rode to the pasture fast enough that dirt continuously spit out from under his tires. He wanted to check the herd and make sure that no cows were missing.

Back at the house, Ginny turned on the television. The national news showed continued riots in the cities over the lack of supplies, the shutdown of government assistance programs and the growing vacuum of leadership at the federal level. The channel flipped through images showing people waiting for hours at ATM machines which only allowed depositors to take out up to $200 a day, an amount that bought very little with inflation rising so fast. Roads were still clogged, often completely impassable with disabled and abandoned vehicles.

Ginny started to turn away but froze when the segment changed. The video footage on the screen showed what the commentators were calling a crisis phenomenon, and from the looks of the carnage, Ginny had to agree. Hordes of people surged down the streets with determination, desperate to escape the cities, and leaving nothing but destrution in their wake. As they moved, they absorbed others who had been stranded along the roads. A reporter had joined the back of one group. He shared images of the homes and businesses ransacked and stripped bare.

Ginny made a mental note to gather the others after lunch to address this problem before it had a chance to get to them. This was another part of the dream she had hoped would not happen. She hoped that the farm was far enough from the cities and major roads that these acts of violence would not reach them.

Brad was late getting back to the house for lunch. When he came out of the laundry room from washing away the dirt and dust, Leah was standing in the kitchen holding out a plate and a cold soda. She had hidden the can in a snug koozie.

"Don't let the kids see you have a soda," she whispered. "They get powdered fruit drink, but I believe anyone who is trying to keep us in food deserves a comfort drink."

Brad smiled and whispered, "Thanks."

He sat at the end of the kitchen island and listened to a group meeting that was just starting at the dining room table. Ginny was talking.

"I want to discuss a report I saw on the television," she said. "They were showing huge groups of people migrating out of the cities toward rural areas. I saw a reporter following a large group out of Greensboro. When he asked someone why they were walking, a man said they couldn't drive anymore. The roads were clogged, there was no gas, and the stores in Greensboro were out of food. So they were heading to rural Virginia to hide out in state and national parks. The small group of friends he was with had seeds and hand tools. They were hoping to find a secluded place where they could plant a garden and build shelters sturdy enough to survive the winter."

Ginny drew a breath and continued. "The national report showed what happens when one of these groups moved through an area. They stripped everything they could find. They overwhelmed towns and neighborhoods. They took food from buildings and gardens, livestock from farms, and they over-hunted everything from rabbits to deer."

"My concern," she said, "is what if a group comes west from Winston or north from Charlotte and ends up here. They could take everything we have, and we wouldn't be able to stop them. How do we prepare for that? I know in the dream we used game fencing, but Brad used what Mr. Thompson left for his own place." Ginny looked at Brad. "I'm not complaining, Brad. You had every right and responsibility to protect what is yours." She looked back to the group. "So, any suggestions?"

Garrett said, "For something that big and that uncontrollable, all we can do is pray and trust God to protect us."

"My barn has a root cellar," Aaron said. "If we see a group coming, we could hide a lot of supplies down there."

"Garrett is right," Mark said. "But I also believe we can make a plan in the meantime. Aaron, that's a great idea. Thanks."

Brad had finished his sandwich and took a long drink of soda to wash it down.

"I have something," he said, setting the can on the counter.

The group looked at him.

"First," he said, "I'm going to poke around my barns and outbuildings to see if there is a hidden root cellar that I don't know about because I like Aaron's plan. Second, I remember the dream, too. In the back of Ginny's barn, I stocked enough posts, tall fencing, and gates to enclose the house, yard, campers, equipment shed, chicken coop, and the barn. I also have enough to enclose part of a pasture. It will be smaller so we will have to be selective about securing the best cattle from our herd, Aaron's herd, and maybe even Tom's. I would like to put Aaron's horses in there as well.

"As you know, it won't stop industrial strength wire cutters, but it will slow them down so maybe we'll have enough time to at least try to stop intruders through diplomacy. If all else fails, well, remember what happened to the motorcycle gang in our dream."

"One more thing," he said. "I have a few solar powered engines that will electrify the fence. I put a few on the fence at my place, but I haven't turned it on. I don't recommend we do that unless we're actually threatened. It's too easy to forget about it, and I don't want anyone to get hurt. Also, I saw evidence of what I think are wild dogs or coyotes on my property. We should get the fence up soon. In the meantime, someone needs to be outside with a shotgun if any of the little ones are playing out there."

"Does anyone else have suggestions?" Mark asked. No one answered. "Then this meeting is adjourned. Continue with whatever you were doing. I need Brad, Aaron and the security team to stay behind."

When everyone went back to their tasks, Mark pulled out a blank piece of paper and roughly sketched an aerial view of the farm. Using that, the group discussed the most strategic way to situate the fencing. When they had made their decisions, Brad and Aaron left to put the post hole diggers on their tractors.

The two men started digging holes near each other at one of the gate sites on the southeast side of the yard. They worked around the planned enclosure in opposite directions until they met on the northern side. As soon as the tractors had finished drilling the holes, everyone paired off to set the posts. By late afternoon, all the posts were in place. Since it was Saturday, they planned to hang the gates and stretch the fencing on Monday.

That afternoon, much to Ginny's relief, her best friend, Jacque Meyers, and her daughter, Melanie Barefoot arrived. Ginny got them settled in her room and introduced them to the group. Jacque and Ginny were as close as sisters and were glad to finally be reunited.

CHAPTER 24
APRIL 22

After dinner, Brad went down to the gun safe in the basement storage area and chose a rifle fitted with a night scope. He brought it upstairs, grabbed an LED flashlight from the office, then walked outside where Mark, Max, Pete, Alex, Sharon and Bennett were gathered around the picnic tables talking.

"Max, Sharon and I will be here waiting for you to call," Mark told Brad. "I want to interrogate whoever you find." He handed Brad one of the two-way radios.

Bennett looked at Brad's flashlight.

"You won't need that." Bennett said as he grinned and handed Brad a set of night vision goggles.

"Sweet. Outdoor store?" Brad asked, grinning.

Bennett nodded. "Employee discount."

Brad laughed. He noticed that Pete and Alex also held night vision goggles.

The sun had set, and there was just enough light for the four men to drive Bennett's pickup to the pasture without using headlights. They parked at the southern end of the pasture opposite where the cows had settled down for the night. Then they climbed to the top of a hill nearby where they could watch the whole lower part of the pasture.

"This is a good spot," Bennett said, looking around. "We're farther from the road than the cows, we have the high ground, and there are no obstructions between us and your herd."

The men settled onto the grass and prepared to wait. There was no talking, and each man watched the herd. A light breeze kept the grass from becoming too damp as they sat watching the stars becoming brighter. When the darkness had completely settled, they put on the night vision goggles. Brad was not prepared for how well he could see.

"Man!" he exclaimed softly. "These are great!"

Bennett chuckled. "I thought so, too. You can't go wrong with the ability to see in the dark."

Three hours after sunset, the men had barely moved when they saw flashlights moving from the road to the pasture.

"This is it," Bennett said quietly.

He had the others spread out and slowly walk toward the herd. Before long, they saw four men climbing over the fence and entering the pasture.

They watched the intruders struggle to single out a small steer, and Bennett whispered orders in the dark. The men knew what to do. They slowly moved toward the herd and saw one of the thieves raise a large knife, aiming it toward the animal. From the angle of the knife, Brad knew it would not be a fatal blow. These men obviously didn't know what they were doing, and their cruelty made Brad angrier. Before the man could bring the weapon down, Brad heard Pete call out through the darkness.

"I wouldn't do that if I were you," Pete yelled. "That steer doesn't belong to you."

The man lowered the knife to his side. The others froze and looked around. They aimed the beams of their flashlights around the pasture, but they couldn't see anyone or determine where the voice was coming from. Two men drew pistols from their holsters.

"Drop your weapons!" Pete yelled. "I'm not the only one pointing a gun at you."

One man angled his gun forward, pointing it toward Pete's voice.

"Freeze!" Pete yelled again. "Drop the weapons."

The pistols and the knife dropped to the ground.

"Turn off your flashlights," Pete ordered. "Step away from the cows."

Three of the men started to walk away from the herd, but the one who had held the knife bent over to retrieve a pistol.

"I did not tell you to pick up that gun," Pete said sternly. "I said to move away from the cows."

All four men stepped away. Brad slipped up behind them and picked up the pistols and the knife.

Pete ordered loudly, "Sit on the ground with your hands behind your back."

The men did as Pete commanded.

"Keep them covered," Pete said loud enough for Brad, Bennett, and Alex to hear.

Pete secured the men's hands with zip ties while Brad took out the radio and called the house.

"Yeah," Mark answered, sounding alert. "Did you get them?"

"Yeah," Brad answered. "Come on down."

A few minutes later they heard a truck coming through the pasture. Mark parked with the headlights shining on the intruders.

"Dwight Hall!" Brad exclaimed with disgust when the deputy's face was illumniated. "What are you doing? Trying to steal my cows? What have I ever done to you? Aren't you supposed to be upholding the law, not breaking it?"

"Brad, you don't have kids," Dwight whined. "You don't know what it's like when your kids are crying because they're hungry. We ran out of food yesterday."

"Who's with you, Dwight?" Brad asked.

"Neighbors."

"Does the sheriff know you're doing this?" Brad asked.

"Hell, no!" Dwight exclaimed. "He'd fire me if he did. Sheriff's a good man. He wouldn't stand for this. He's trying to keep the county calm and safe."

"That's good to hear," mumbled Mark.

"Where's your truck, Dwight?" Brad asked.

"On the road, behind the trees," Dwight answered sullenly.

"Give me your keys," Brad said.

"Aw, Brad, don't take my truck!" Dwight whined.

"I'm not," Brad said. "But all of you are going to walk home. I will leave your truck at the end of the road tomorrow. Then you go to Elkin. We heard the Baptist church has a soup kitchen. Your family can eat one meal a day there. If there's any food left over, maybe you can take some home. And Dwight, you'd better start a garden. This is going to last a long time, probably a lot longer than any of us thought. You and your neighbors need to work together. Can you do that?"

"Maybe," Dwight said sullenly.

"No maybes, Dwight," Brad said sternly, shaking his head. "You said it yourself. You have kids to take care of. You have no choice if you want them to survive. If you steal from the wrong farmer, you'll be dead, and your family will never know what happened to you. After that, who's going to protect them? So, you don't get to say maybe. You're going to have to do the work, start a garden and figure out how to feed them on your own. Do you understand?"

Dwight was quiet.

"I understand," one of the men said. "I told him this was stupid. We can start a garden. If Dwight won't work to grow food, he won't eat."

"Dwight," Brad said, "I won't tell the sheriff this time, but if I find out you're doing this again, I will let him know. Where did you get the drones?"

"Another neighbor," Dwight said quietly. "We all shared the meat."

Brad turned to Mark, "Move the truck so the lights point out to the road."

When Mark had done that, Brad cut the ties off their hands. "Okay. Go. I'll leave the truck at the end of the road sometime tomorrow."

Dwight said nothing. He and two others turned and walked away.

The last man said, "Thank you. You could've shot us and our families would never have known what happened to us. I'll get the neighbors together, and we'll plant a community garden." He paused. "Dwight's a lazy bum. I should've never listened to him."

"If he starts this up again," Brad said, "call the sheriff. Do not go out to help him."

"I know," the man said then turned and walked away.

"Do you think Dwight will listen?" Mark asked Brad.

"No," Brad answered. "He won't even try. He's too lazy to be smart. Once he realizes how much work it is to grow food, he'll do something stupid and end up getting killed, and then where will his kids be?"

They watched the flashlight beams of the thieves until they reached the road and turned to follow it north.

"Come on, let's go back," Brad said. "I'm tired and disgusted."

It was just after midnight when the men carried their gear to the truck and headed back to the house. They could still get a couple hours of sleep before dawn and another day of work.

As evening settled in, Tina watched the men load the truck and drive out toward the pasture. She sat outside her camper, replaying her conversations with Brad and picturing his easy smile and kind eyes. Worry for Brad tugged at her, but she didn't say anything. She wasn't family, just a guest brought along by a friend's family, and she didn't want to overstep.

She tried to stay quiet and out of the way, but that was becoming harder whenever Brad was around. He never made her feel like an outsider. He noticed her, listened to her, and made her feel welcome at the farm. He was, without question, the most handsome, capable man she had ever met. She found herself comparing him to the boys back home who liked to play tough. She wondered if they were able to survive, let alone thrive, in a situation like this the way Brad did.

The minutes ticked by slowly, and the night grew chilly. Tina went inside the camper, but she couldn't sleep because she was so worried for Brad. After a few hours of tossing and turning, she heard another truck start behind the barn and heard it's rumble head toward the pastures. Tina clung anxiously to her sheets as she prayed everything was all right.

A while later she heard the trucks return. She heard the deep and familiar voices of the men as they talked softly in the back yard. Everything must be okay, and she finally felt herself relax. Relieved, she fell asleep.

Brad glanced at Tina's camper as he turned to go inside the house. He hoped she was sleeping soundly. Inside the house, he showered and got ready for bed, though he was unsure if he would fall asleep. He was wired, and he was angry. Stupid people who were too lazy to work could undermine everything he and his family had done to ensure their survival. Brad started a movie on his tablet to help him relax and forget his anger. Before long, he was asleep.

CHAPTER 25

APRIL 23

North Carolina, USA

Brad yawned and got up. It was still dark, but he hadn't been able to sleep well after the events in the pasture. He walked into the kitchen and started the coffee. Standing in a daze, Brad watched the coffee slowly drip into the carafe. Finally, he poured himself a cup of the hot liquid then looked into the den, surprised to see Bennett sitting at the computer.

"Bennett, do you want some coffee?" Brad asked. "I can't believe you maintained your shift after spending part of the night in the pasture.

Bennett raised his empty cup. "Please." His eyes never left the screen. "I couldn't sleep, so I figured I'd just watch the monitor."

"Yeah, I know what you mean," Brad said as he walked the carafe of hot coffee to the den. He refilled Bennett's cup. "I couldn't sleep either. Everything quiet?"

"For now," Bennett replied.

Brad took the carafe back to the kitchen and toasted a slice of Donna's homemade bread.

"I'm going out to the pasture. I want to check the cows. I need to make sure every single one of them is there and healthy."

"I get it," Bennett said. "I'll tell the others where you went."

Brad grabbed a flashlight and walked to the equipment shed. He decided to take the golf cart. People were still sleeping in the campers, and he didn't want to wake anyone by starting a truck or the four-wheeler. Just as he turned the key in the cart, a news report flashed across the screen of his cellphone. Brad felt this stomach drop. What now? He knew any news this early in the morning couldn't be good. He got his phone and began to read.

The terrorists had hit more targets. They had detonated bombs in Manhattan, Atlanta, San Francisco, Miami, and Chicago. Power plants in New York, Ohio and Pennsylvania had been damaged along with steel plants across the midwest. Cargo ships off the coasts opened hidden missile launchers. They destroyed San Diego Harbor, Boston Harbor, and Tacoma Harbor. Terrorists driving speed boats used portable missile launchers to bring down more bridges over major rivers.

Brad shook his head and started driving the golf cart. It was just like the dream.

The sun had burst over the horizon, and the sky had gone from gray to vibrant Carolina blue when Brad spotted the cows. He stopped the cart at the top of the hill where they had parked last night. Some of the cows were still lying down in the grass, some were up and grazing, and some were standing in the creek drinking. The new bull was nursing its mother and seemed to be growing at an astonishing rate.

Brad sighed. In a few days this area would have a high game fence around it and there would be horses included. How would he decide which of his cows got the protection and which ones would be left to the thieves, dogs, and coyotes? The donkeys would stay outside the game fence. They would keep the other livestock safe from a dog or coyote, but not even donkeys could fight armed humans trying to get food.

Brad walked through the herd inspecting the cows. The new little bull hid behind his mother until Brad got nearer. Then he approached Brad with the bravado that would someday scare people, but for now, it was humorous. Brad chuckled and rubbed the calf on the head. This was soothing after last night. He didn't like confrontation, but he wouldn't run from it. He wasn't made for the life of a police officer or a soldier; he was a farmer. This land was where he belonged.

Brad drove the golf cart to his farm to check on the house and the buildings. He remembered it was Sunday and looked at his watch. Garrett would be setting up the yard for the church service. On impulse he drove the cart across the yard, avoiding the spikes in the driveway, turned onto the road and headed to the Smith house.

When Brad drove up to the house, no one heard him coming because the cart was silent compared to the noise of the trucks or four-wheeler. He knocked on the door then heard running and whispering inside. He felt bad that he had taken them by surprise.

Rob Smith came to the door.

"Brad!" he exclaimed. He looked surprised and relieved that it was a neighbor. "What can I do for you?"

"I'm sorry to bother you," Brad said. "I should have just called. I was out checking the herd and decided to invite you to the church service Garrett is having this morning."

Rob thought for a moment. "How would we get there? Your driveway would blow out our tires."

"It will start in about fifteen minutes," Brad said. "I can take anyone who wants to go on the golf cart."

"Let me check," Rob said and walked back into the house.

Rob came back to the door. "It will be just Robbie, Amanda and me. The others don't want to go."

"Sounds good," Brad said. "I'll wait."

Brad walked back to the cart and called Garrett. He told Garrett he was bringing Robert and his children to the service. Garrett said they would wait.

When Brad drove the Smith family through the farm roads that led back to the house, Rob was astonished at the amount of people waiting in the yard at the Reed farm. Garrett came over, welcomed him and introduced him to the adults. Brad walked Robbie and Amanda to the other kids and introduced them. Bonnie and Hannah immediately pulled Amanda with them to find seats. Caleb and Bobby slid apart at one of the picnic tables to make room for Robbie to sit with them.

Garrett started the service with a welcome and a prayer of thanks. The lesson was on strength and peace that comes only from God. In their current situation, Brad appreciated every word.

After the service, Ginny invited Rob and the children to stay for a lunch of casseroles and salad. After they ate, the children wanted to stay and play. Rob wanted to get back to his garden, so Brad drove him back to the Smith house with the promise to have his children back by five o'clock or before.

When Brad parked the golf cart next to Rob's truck, Sarah came out of the house. Jack followed closely behind her.

"Where are my children?" she asked, frowning.

"I let them stay and play with the others," Rob said. "I thought it would be good for them to spend time with kids their age."

"Without my permission?" Sarah asked testily.

"You weren't there, Sarah," he said. "I heard them laughing for the first time since all of this started. They're safe and will have a good time."

"I want to go play," Abby said from the front porch.

"No," Jack said, turning back to the porch to look at Abby. "It's not safe."

Brad bristled. "Jack, I can assure you it's very safe. She would have a good time."

"Jack," Rob said, "Abby needs friends her age just like my kids do and just like the rest of us adults need friends. I've seen the place and met the adults and children. It will be a good experience for her. I think it would be good for all of you, too."

Marley came out the door and walked up to Brad. "May Abby and I go back with you? I wasn't ready this morning, but I would like to meet your family."

"Marley!" Jack yelled. "No."

Marley turned to Jack. "This time I'm making the decision. I'll see you later this afternoon." She took Abby's hand, and they went to the golf cart with Brad.

When Brad returned to the farm with Marley and Abby, Mark and Ginny greeted them. Mark introduced Marley to the adults, and Ginny took Abby to play with Haley, Riley and Geeta.

Brad sat in a lawn chair under the oak trees watching the kids. The teenagers were playing cornhole while Brute and Barf begged for attention. The younger boys were taking turns on the tire swing, and the little girls had made a playhouse with yarn tied around some smaller trees. It was a good afternoon.

Brad heard, "May I sit here?"

He looked up to see Tina pointing to the empty chair beside him and immediately straightened up in his own chair.

"Sure," he said.

"You seem very introspective today," Tina said. "Last night really bothered you didn't it."

"Yes, it did," Brad said, nodding. "I still need to take Dwight's truck to the end of the road. Would you mind going with me? You can follow me in my truck and bring me back."

"Sure," Tina said. "I would like to do that."

Brad told Mark what he and Tina were doing and that he should be back in time to take Marley and the kids home. They got into Brad's truck, and he drove through the farm lanes until he came to the clinic.

"This is Ginny's clinic," Brad told her. "It's the only way we can access the highway now.

"I like the commute," Tina said.

Brad smiled. "She does too. I'm surprised Dwight's truck isn't here. It's the closest point from the road to the pasture. He turned right onto the paved road and drove slowly, looking for Dwight's truck. It was on the shoulder of the road between the clinic and his farmhouse.

Brad stopped the truck and got out. Tina ran around the front of it and slid into the driver's seat, preparing to follow him. Brad drove Dwight's truck to the stop sign, eased it onto the shoulder, and left the keys in the console before heading back.

Tina had parked and moved to the passenger's seat when Brad walked back to his truck. He got in, turned around and headed back toward the clinic. When they passed his farm, Brad slowed, studying the front of his house.

"What is that place?" Tina asked, pointing to the house.

"That used to be the Thompson's place, but I bought it," he replied. "The sale was finalized right before all this happened."

"It looks sad," Tina said. "Why is it boarded up and surrounded by a fence?"

"Because it's empty," Brad replied. "We boarded up the windows and doors like we did at Aaron's. It's not as close to the road as Aaron's house, but it's still visible. I've already had one group of people trying to live in it, so I'm glad I put the game fence around it and spiked the driveway. There are cameras here, too; we monitor them from Ginny's house."

"Did you ever live here?" Tina asked.

"No," He accelerated, heading back toward Ginny's. "We settled the sale on March 30th. They didn't move out until April 10th, when North Korea launched that missile. I hadn't even seen the inside of the house until last week."

"Could I see it?" she asked as they reached the clinic.

Brad looked at her with surprise. "You want to see an old farmhouse?"

"Yes."

Brad looked at his watch. "Okay. We have time."

Brad turned into the clinic parking lot, then crossed Ginny's farm until he turned onto a newly cut path. He drove carefully and stopped behind his barn.

"I usually park here so no one can see the truck from the road," he said.

They got out of the truck. Brad unlocked the gate and led them through the fence, closing the gate behind them. He pointed to the equipment shed.

"That's where all the equipment that came with the farm is stored. Do you want to see that? There are some pretty cool old pieces in there."

"Yes, but the house first, in case we run out of time," she answered.

Brad unlocked the screen door and they walked into the back porch. While he was unlocking the back door, Tina wandered. She touched the cold metal of the hand pump on the sink near the door. She ran her hand along the scarred wooden table, its surfaced nicked from years of hard work. She pushed against the top of an old rocking chair with a braided seat and smiled when it creaked.

Brad watched Tina move slowly through each room of the house, taking everything in. She didn't look like she was seeing it for the first time. It was like she was remembering, like she was coming home.

Thank you for bringing me here," Tina said after she had seen all the rooms. "It's lovely. It's sad you haven't gotten to live here yet."

"You like the house?" he asked, sounding surprised.

"Yes. It reminds me of two houses I've been in, one of which was my grandparents'."

"And the other?" Brad asked as he locked the door behind him and they walked back to the truck.

Tina climbed into the passenger's seat. She didn't answer Brad's question.

Instead, she asked, "Will you tell me about the dream everyone talks about?"

Brad was surprised. He forgot that not everyone living at the farm had experienced the phenomenon of having the same dream. As Brad drove back to the house, he told her about how he and his siblings had the same exact dream and how some of the others had a more limited version of the dream.

"Was that house in your dream?" she asked.

"No," Brad said. "Why?"

"Because I had a dream, too," Tina said, then hesistated for a moment. "It was nothing like yours. I dreamed I was on a farm that I had never been to before, and a national crisis had taken place. In the dream I worked hard, planting, harvesting, and preserving food. But I was very content.

"When I woke up, a heavy burden sat on my chest. I knew I had to get ready for something, but I didn't know what. I went shopping. I stuffed large bags with shoes, coats, clothing, toiletries, and protein bars. The day the missile was launched, I was terrified. I knew I wasn't supposed to be in Huntersville, but I had no idea where I was to go. When Grace asked me to come with her, I didn't hesitate for a second, and you know the rest of my story from there."

Brad was stunned. She was the first person he had met, not from their area or their group, who had been warned in a dream. Granted, it was different from his, but still, she had been forewarned, too.

"Are you sure it was that house?" he asked.

"Yes," she said. "I knew every room there. I even knew the pump's handle over the sink on the back porch because I used it in my dream. The handle sticks slightly when you get to the bottom, and you have to pull it gently to get it to go back up. I know that the third door in the kitchen leads to the pantry that has steps going down to a root cellar style basement."

"We didn't go in there," Brad said, "and yet you know that?"

Tina smiled. "I kept potatoes, onions, apples, pears, and canned food in there. In the dream, I mean."

"Why haven't you mention your dream when you heard us talking about ours?" he asked.

Tina shrugged. "Because I didn't make the connection to this place until right now. I thought I was still waiting to get to where I was supposed to be."

They arrived at the house and Brad stopped the truck behind the equipment shed. He stared at the steering wheel, trying to make sense of what she had just told him. Tina opened the passenger door to get out.

"I own that farm," Brad said, stopping Tina before she got out of the truck. "Was I in your dream?"

She turned back to Brad. "Yes."

Tina got out of the truck, leaving Brad staring at her, eyes wide and his mouth hanging open. He jumped out of the truck and caught up with her, gently taking her elbow to slow her down.

"You can't just leave me hanging after a statement like that," he said. "What were you and I doing at the farm?"

"We were working. Very hard, actually," she said, looking around then back at him. "I don't know the time frame in reference to where we are now, but it was summer, and we were working very hard to get enough food preserved for the winter."

"Did we talk? Did we live there?" Brad asked.

"We talked, but I don't know if we lived there. It was a short dream."

"What did we talk about?" he asked.

Tina chuckled. "We talked about which foods were ripe and if we had enough jar lids for the canning."

"That's it?"

"Brad," she said, "it wasn't a long, detailed dream like you and your siblings had. It was short and left me with more questions than answers, but I do know it left me with the very distinct image of that farm."

"Why didn't you tell me when you first got here?" he asked.

"Brad, think about it. I was a stranger in a strange place. You didn't know me, and I certainly didn't know you. During the first week I was here, I barely talked, except when I was teaching. My whole purpose until this moment has been to teach, keep quiet, and remain invisible so I wouldn't make anyone angry and ask me to leave. I was confused. I felt safe here, and I wanted to stay. Plus, until now, I still hadn't found the farm I was looking for."

"You thought we would make you leave?" Brad asked.

"Don't get offended," Tina said, trying to reassure him. "We didn't know each other before that missile launched. My whole life had been completely uprooted and turned upside down. You were still in the place you knew, where you were comfortable, and most importantly, where you were in control. I've been completely out of control. I've felt like I was bouncing around like a ball in a pinball machine just hoping I didn't fall into the hole. Do you blame me for being quiet? What was I supposed to do, go up to you and say, 'Hey, I'm Tina and you are the man in my dream. Where's my farm?' You would have thought I was completely bonkers."

"I'm so sorry you have felt that way," Brad said, loosening his grip on her arm. "No wonder you were crying behind the barn. Tina, no one would make you leave. You've become an important part of this group."

"Thank you," Tina said with a soft smile. "I no longer feel that way. I just felt that way in the beginning. I know that I have a place here now. I enjoy teaching the different age groups, helping Erica, Leah and Barbara with the meals, and even the cleanup and laundry. I feel like this is a family, even if we aren't all related."

"I need to help Erica with dinner," Tina said, walking toward the back door. "But there is one thing missing on that farm."

"What?" Brad asked.

Tina grinned, pausing to look back at him. "The dairy cow in the barn that hits me with her tail when I milk her."

Tina turned and walked to the house, but she heard Brad say to himself, "Dairy cow?"

Grinning, Tina walked into the kitchen.

Erica turned when she saw Tina. "Hey. I wondered where you were. I haven't seen you all afternoon. Are you okay?"

"I'm fine," Tina answered. "I helped Brad move the truck that belonged to the men who tried to steal his cow. Then he showed me his farmhouse."

"You got to see Brad's house?" Erica asked. "I've heard them talking about it, and I've been dying to see it. What did it look like?"

Tina described the old farmhouse, the buildings and the sad look the plywood and fence gave it.

"It should be a happy, thriving place," Tina said. "Not one that looks abandoned and derelict. It's not Brad's fault the world as we knew it ended. He was smart to do what he did. I just feel sorry for the place."

Dinner was a mixture of sandwiches and leftovers from the past several days. Sunday suppers were becoming the meal when the refrigerator was cleaned out before the new week. No food was wasted.

Marley and the kids were invited to eat dinner. As soon as they were finished, Brad took them back to their house. He noticed the kids were quiet on the ride back. He thought they were probably sad to leave the new friends they had found.

Marley turned and saw Amanda was crying.

"Amanda! What's wrong?" she asked.

"Aunt Marley, I don't want to go back," Amanda said. "It's miserable at our house. Mom and Uncle Jack don't do anything but complain while you and Dad do all the work. It was fun back there. I like Bonnie and Hannah. I like the boys, too. Hannah said there's a boy from another farm that comes for classes in the mornings. Can we go to the school, too?"

"I'm going to talk to Jack and your parents," Marley said, "You should be getting an education."

When they got to the house, Marley thanked Brad for a lovely afternoon.

"If you want the kids to come to classes," Brad said, "have Rob call Mark. They can discuss how the kids will get there. Probably through the gate behind the clinic."

"Thank you, Brad," Marley said. "I'm sure he will be calling you soon." She and the kids waved at Brad as he left.

Rob came out of the house and walked up to Marley. "Well, how did the kids do?"

Marley turned to Rob. "I want them to go to the school. Today is the first day they have laughed since we got here."

Rob told the kids to go into the house then turned back to Marley.

"You're right," he said. "It would be good for them."

"Amanda cried because she didn't want to come back here," Marley said. "She was very critical of Sarah and Jack."

" I know," Rob sighed. "Those two aren't coping well at all. Let's go inside and discuss this. I want to call Mark and arrange for the kids to go to school."

CHAPTER 26

APRIL 24

Switzerland

John Rosen called a meeting of The Committee and the representatives of the cooperating countries. He took his place at the head of the chalet's long dining room table. The twelve chairs around it were full, and the aides lined the walls in deep, comfortable chairs. George sat in a lone chair by the door, positioned like a sentry.

"Gentlemen," John began, his voice steady, "as planned, the last several days have been difficult for the United States. We are now entering the next phase of our global plan. China is acquiring Taiwan and pushing farther into the South China Sea." He looked at Mr. Lin, "Expect pushback from the Asian countires, but don't get overly concerned. Much of the U.S. Military is being pulled out of the area. They are so consumed with their own domestic problems that they cannot afford to support Taiwan, Japan, South Korea, or the Philippines."

Rosen shifted his attention to the representative from Russia. "Your next step is expansion beyond Ukraine into Eastern Europe. Expect pushback from NATO, minus the United States. I imagine the U.S. is annoyed that NATO hasn't come to their aid in any way since

April 10th."

He paused, letting out a long, slow breath. "Let me remind every-one of our agreement. No nuclear weapons. There's no use reshaping the world if we destroy the world in the process."

A ripple of nods moved around the table.

"Also," Rosen continued, turning back to Mr. Lin. "China is not to encroach on India. India will be allowed to move into Pakistan, Nepal, and Bangladesh." His eyes swept the room. "Be patient. Once we secure our positions in Europe and Asia, we can consolidate control in Africa and South America."

Rosen caught the faint, satisfied smiles from the Brazilian and South African representatives.

After answering a round of questions, John adjourned the meeting. He nodded discreetly to George who stood and opened the doors to the foyer. The room emptied with the soft rustle of belongings and murmured farewells. John and George watched the procession disappear into the night.

"Surveillance protocols are in place," George said. He held up his phone. Blinking lights crawled across the map of Davos. "We should have the car recordings shortly."

"Good," John said, a thin smile forming. "I'm curious how they will report this to their governments, especially Mr. Lin. He did not like today's boundaries. China failed to control North Korea, and now he's lost the territory he wanted around India." John's smile sharpened. "Well, too bad for Mr. Lin. They shouldn't have promised what they couldn't deliver."

George's phone buzzed with incoming messages. The two men turned back toward the study, ready to listen to the recordings taken from inside the departing cars.

North Carolina, USA

Sunlight filtered through the kitchen curtains when Brad walked in for breakfast. He saw several people already crowded around the television, drinking coffee and talking softly.

"What's happened now?" he asked Ginny, who was standing in the back of the crowd.

"After absorbing Taiwan, China is systematically claiming more islands in the South China Sea," Ginny told him. "Russia has established its government in Ukraine and placed troops along all its borders with the eastern European countries. Iran has declared war on Israel." She paused. "That seems to have happened very fast, like Russia and China were ready and waiting."

She continued, "Rioting continues across the country. Supply chains are disrupted because the bridges across the major rivers were damaged or blown apart, and ports are damaged, which complicates the importation of supplies. Also, the steam plant south of here was vandalized last night. I don't know what that means for us in the way of electrical service."

Brad thought for a moment. "I hope the southeastern pipeline is still intact. That's how we get our gasoline."

"It must be," Ginny said. "It hasn't been mentioned."

"Good," Brad murmured, and he turned toward the kitchen when Mike announced breakfast was ready.

After breakfast, the men worked on getting the tall fence installed along the fence posts they'd set two days earlier. Robert pulled the teenagers out of school to help plant the garden. Rain was in the forecast, and he wanted the seeds in the ground. Most of the women also helped with the planting.

By mid afternoon, the fence was finished, and the garden was planted. Covered in dirt and dripping with sweat, Brad wanted nothing more than a shower and a glass of something cold to drink. Everyone was hot, tired, and dirty when they trudged back to the house. They left their dirty shoes and boots in the mudroom, then drifted toward the kitchen, where several people stood in line waiting to pour themselves a cup of cold water from the refrigerator.

Brad ended up last. When his turn finally came, his cup was only half full when the power went out and the water stopped. The kitchen lights blinked off, and the room fell silent.

Ginny started giving orders. "Everyone take a room! Unplug everything and flip off any light switches. The generator will come on in a few seconds, but we need to conserve fuel."

Adults and teenagers scattered across the house and campers, checking switches and appliances. Then everyone assembled outside.

"I guess this is it for electricity," Mark said.

"Grilled hamburgers for supper," Leah said. "I was going to use the hamburger for spaghetti sauce, but it seems we have a change of plans."

"I just want a shower," whined Bonnie, brushing her hair back from her face.

"The generator is running the pump, but we can't use the showers like normal," Ginny told her with a soft, sympathetic voice. "There is soap at the pump house, and you can use the outdoor shower. We will just have to be quick about it, so everyone can get their turn."

Ginny turned to Adam. "Can you guys check online for any information about the power outage? Our power company is a co-op called Rural Electric. It's primary source of electricity is Royal Energy, which is south of us."

After listening to the conversations in the yard, Brad took off his shirt and washed at the pump in the back yard. He was still hot, and the cold water felt good against his skin.

Tina came out of the camper in a swimsuit with the intention of going to the outdoor shower. She walked around the camper and stopped. Brad stood at the pump house with his shirt off, rinsing soap from his upper body.

Tina watched Brad's biceps bulge as he moved his arms. His stomach was flat with defined abdominal muscles. To her he looked like a Michelangelo sculpture. When she realized she was staring, she hurriedly turned and entered the outdoor shower. It took two of the containers of water to make her feel halfway clean, but it was better than what she had felt before. As she toweled herself dry, she wondered if this would be her hygiene in the future.

Brad had seen Tina in his peripheral vision. He was amused and flattered that she had stopped to watch him. He turned slightly so he could see her in her swimsuit. She was compact and slim, but she had great curves that he hadn't noticed when she was wearing her normal clothes. Tina didn't wear the tight, form fitting clothes that a lot of women her age did. Even Ginny wore leggings and yoga pants.

As he was rinsing, he saw Tina turn and go to the outdoor shower. When Brad was finished, he dried off with his shirt and walked to the house with a grin on his face. He couldn't suppress the smile, and he wasn't sure why.

The other men and teenage boys followed Brad's lead at the hand pump. One of the other girls managed to use the third container of warm water in the outdoor shower. Garrett started a fire in the fire pit, put a grate over it and placed pots of water on it to heat. When it was warm enough, the women refilled the outdoor shower bags and a few of them were able to take limited showers.

By dinner, everyone had been able to clean enough of the dirt and sweat off to feel more comfortable. They were all outside eating the hamburgers and hotdogs that had been cooked on the grill.

Leah, Barbara, Robert and Garrett were brainstorming the best way to cook meals outside over the open fire if power outages became more frequent. Ginny and Donna were trying to decide the best way to can the produce from the garden if they didn't have a stove top.

Suddenly the generator went quiet. Ginny looked up. The back door light was on.

She stood. "Everyone grab a shower while you can, and recharge your electronics. Be sparing with the hot water, though. There are a lot of us."

Brad remembered the limits of the hot water heater from growing up with three siblings and knew that the last ones to shower would probably end up with cold water. He got up and walked into the house. No one was in the laundry room shower, so he leaned out the back door and motioned to Tina to join him.

"Use this one," he said when she came into the house. "No one is in here."

"You go first, then I'll use it," she said. "I had a better rinse in the outdoor shower than you did at the pump house. And don't argue, I insist. I'll wait for you."

Brad agreed. He took a quick shower then came out to let Tina shower. Brad went back out to the yard and helped Ginny clear the food from the tables and carry it back into the house. People would be coming back for seconds since their meal had been interrupted. He left the last of the condiments on the island and hurried back out the door when he heard Ginny ask Mark and Pete to start on the dirty dishes while she showered.

Tina was sitting in a lawn chair watching the teenagers play cornhole as the sunlight disappeared. Brad dropped down in the chair beside her.

"You said my house reminded you of your grandparents'. Did you grow up on a farm?" he asked.

"Yes, I did," Tina answered. "We had about three hundred acres. Dad grew corn, wheat, and soybeans. We had four poultry houses and raised chickens for a local processing plant. Dad had a nice herd of Hereford cattle. The garden plot was about two acres, and there were groups of fruit trees, muscadines, scuppernongs, blueberries, raspberries, and elderberries.

Brad heard the fondness in her voice as she told him about her family's farm. It was no wonder she had adapted well here. She was used to the type of work they were doing.

"How did you end up teaching in Huntersville?" he asked.

"There were no jobs in my area, and Mecklenburg County was begging for teachers," she said. My family wasn't happy that I was moving so close to Charlotte. All they knew about the area was the bad news they occasionally saw on the television." She chuckled. "In my suitcase is a 9mm pistol with an extra magazine and two boxes of bullets. Dad insisted I have that when I told them I was moving so close to Charlotte."

"I'm guessing you know how to use it." Brad said.

"Yes," she said, smiling. "Guns were a normal part of life growing up. There was always someone going hunting, or we were joining in the contests at the gun range Dad organized for us."

Tina grinned. "I actually know how to cook on that wood stove in your house. That's all my grandmother had, and I stayed with them a lot while I was in college. They were getting frail and needed help. I commuted to school, stayed with them, and they paid part of my tuition. If the power goes out for good, maybe we can take the produce over to your place for canning."

"That's a good idea," Brad said. "I'll remember that."

He and Tina talked until the sun was gone. They spoke about a variety of topics until the yard was empty and the darkness crept in to cool the night air.

CHAPTER 27

APRIL 25

North Carolina, USA

Everyone was in the dining room, talking between bites of egg burritos when Ginny stood up. The room got quiet as everyone put down forks and mugs and turned their attention to her.

"Everyone, I have an announcement," she said.

Ginny gestured to Pete, who stood from the chair beside hers and took her hand.

"I asked Ginny to marry me," he said, "and she said yes."

The kitchen and dining room erupted into clapping and cheers. Everyone jumped up to wish the couple congratulations. Brad wondered if this was one of the reasons Garrett rushed to get ordained, so he could marry them. The women immediately started asking about dates and plans. The celebration was interrupted when Ginny's phone rang.

"This is Dr. Reed," she said. Everyone watched as her smile disappeared into a worried frown. "When did this happen?" She paused. "I understand. Put pressure on the wound and take him to my clinic. I'll meet you there." She ended the call.

"Dwight Hall was shot just a few minutes ago trying to steal another steer," she said, moving away from the table. "Daniel Speaks and his brother-in-law are taking him to the clinic. He's evidently bleeding badly." She looked at Jacque, Sharon and Erica. "Grab the emergency supply packs; get several and meet me at my truck."

Within a minute, the four women were in the truck and driving through the farm lanes to the clinic. Mark, Pete, Alex, Garrett and Max followed in Mark's truck. Brad tried to decide if he should go about his work on the farm or follow the others to the clinic. The clinic won. He got on the four-wheeler and followed the trucks bouncing along the farm lanes.

When Brad got to the clinic, Dwight had already been carried into the surgery area. He thrashed on the metal examination table, screaming, and Jacque struggled to get close enough to assess his wound. Pete, Alex, Garrett and Max fought to keep him still. Erica cut away Dwight's pants leg, exposing the bullet hole in Dwight's thigh that was still bleeding.

"I think the bullet hit an artery," Jacque said, "but not a main one or he would already be dead."

Several years as a medic in the army gave Sharon a quiet confidence as she pulled off her belt and wrapped it around his thigh at the groin. She pulled as tight as she could and fastened it. Dwight screamed in pain and passed out, but the bleeding slowed.

Brad watched Jacque direct Ginny, Sharon and Erica as they tried to help Dwight. Pete, Alex, Garrett and Max continued their hold on his body. The door to the reception area was open. Through the windows, Brad saw Mark talking with Daniel and his brother-in-law, Blake Stevens. Brad went out the front door and listened. He saw disgust in Daniel's eyes as he spoke.

"Dwight was sneaking into my pasture," Daniel said. "I knew what he was after, because Tom Sutton had warned me. Blake and I went out on the porch, and I yelled at him to get off my property and go home. He didn't listen. I told him again to turn around and leave. The idiot pulled his pistol and shot at us. The bullet missed me by only a few inches and is embedded in the column at the side of the porch. I was armed; I always am. So I fired back. I aimed at his leg because I didn't want to kill him. I meant to get his lower leg, but he moved. When we saw how badly he was bleeding, I called the Doc because it didn't seem like we had enough time to get him to the hospital in Elkin."

"We need to call the sheriff," Mark said.

"I already did," Daniel said, holding up a hand. "I told him what happened and that we were going to Doc Reed's clinic. He should be here before long."

As if on cue, Sheriff Cochran drove into the parking lot at the clinic. He parked and crossed the lot toward them, gravel crunching under the weight of his heavy boots. At fifty years old, Steven Cochran stood six feet tall, with a slim, but solidly built frame. He had been sheriff for almost ten years. Known for his fairness, common sense, and ethical behavior, he easily won reelection and probably would for as long as he wanted to keep the job.

The sheriff shook hands with Daniel, Mark, and Brad, and Daniel introduced him to Blake. Brad listened while Daniel and Blake described what happened. Mark added that Brad caught Dwight sneaking into their pasture and stopped him just before he killed a steer. He also told the sheriff that Tom Sutton's game cameras captured Dwight sneaking into his pasture and that one of Tom's steers had been butchered.

The sheriff shook his head in disgust. "I'm not surprised. I've tried and tried to help that boy, hoping he would develop a work ethic, but I think he's a hopeless cause. The sad part is that his wife and kids will be the ones to suffer for this."

Ginny leaned out the front door of the clinic.

"Sheriff, we got the bleeding stopped, but Jacque can't do anything else for him here. He needs a hospital," she said, wiping sweat from her eyes with her forearm. "Can you make that happen?"

Sheriff Cochran stepped a few paces away to make a phone call. When he ended the call, he walked back to the group.

"An ambulance is on the way," he said. "It's probably the only one still working. Will he live?"

"I don't know, Sheriff," Ginny answered. "He's lost a lot of blood, and there's grass and debris in the wound. He's wounded too severely for us to try any further medical care. He needs anesthesia and a surgeon. Even if he survives, he will most likely have an infection to worry about."

A few minutes later the ambulance pulled into the now-crowded clinic parking lot. The paramedics went inside, loaded an unconscious Dwight onto the stretcher and brought him back out to the ambulance. Once he was secured, the driver turned on the flashing lights and sped toward Elkin.

"I guess it's up to me to go tell Marylee about her husband," the sheriff said with a sigh.

"Dwight's truck is parked on the side of the road near my pasture," Daniel said. "I took his keys from his pocket. If you'll come that way, I'll follow you in it so she can have a way to get around. Blake can follow us and take me back home."

"We can do that," the sheriff replied. "I have to write a report on this, Daniel, but I'm not going to file any charges. Dwight was trespassing, and he fired first."

"I appreciate that, Sheriff," Daniel replied, looking grateful.

Brad and Mark watched Sheriff Cochran and Daniel leave the parking lot. Ginny, Jacque, Erica, Sharon, Pete and Max came out of the clinic carrying the bloodied drapes and bandages. Ginny placed the trash in a metal barrel and set it on fire.

"That's the only way we have to deal with hazardous waste; burn it," she said, looking at the group.

Pete stood beside her, waiting for the fire in the barrel to burn itself out. They watched the rest of the group climb onto the back of Mark's truck to ride back to the house.

Brad walked over to them.

"You and Jacque did good, Ginny," Brad said before he got back on the four-wheeler. "Our efforts kept Daniel Sparks and Hank Miller safe. I hate Dwight was shot, but he's the cause of his own problems."

"You're right," Ginny said, leaning against the four-wheeler. "I'm glad the dreams changed and the other two are safe."

When Brad got back to the house, he saw that Tina had the high school students outside at the picnic tables working on different math problems. He was surprised but glad to see Amanda Smith had joined the group, and Brady Sutton was back. Evidently things were slow enough at the Johnson farm that Carson had been released for classes as well. He walked into the house to see Garrett watching the news network from Atlanta.

"What's going on?" Brad asked.

Garrett pointed to the screen. Brad saw images of rubble where buildings once stood. Reporters from outside the city showed images of smoke hanging heavily over the urban skylines.

"Those are pictures of the cities that were hit with bombs overnight. More detonated in New York, Chicago, Los Angeles, and Washington DC. People are sending drones over the areas. Bombs in Manhattan destroyed the United Nations Building, Wall Street and parts of Fifth Avenue. Washington DC was hit hard. They sent the President, Vice President, Cabinet, Congress and the Supreme Court justices into undisclosed locations, probably that network of bunkers that people say are in the Blue Ridge Mountains."

Garrett continued, "A lot of the oil refineries in Houston are gone, but not all. We may have all the gas we'll get for a long time. I hope Aaron has harnesses and wagons for his horses. They said to expect electrical blackouts more often than we have service. They're diverting electricity to areas that have none so crews can get their equipment back online."

"I don't know where our government is," Garrett said with disgust, "but they're completely silent. No one has heard from them since the latest round of bombings. They're just letting people in the cities kill each other over food. Most cities now have a vacuum of leadership, and gangs are taking over. In some cases, the gangs are fighting each other over turf and supplies. No one seems to be able to stop the terrorists or find their bombs before they're detonated. It's complete chaos."

Mark had walked up behind them and was watching the report.

"I think we need to call another group meeting," he said. "The kids can play outside since the fence is up." He looked at his brother. "Garrett, you have solar panels and batteries in the shed, right?"

"Yes," Garrett replied. "What are you thinking?"

Mark pointed to the screen. The picture showed mass migrations of people moving away from the bombed areas.

"Between that and power outages, we need a new plan," he said and turned around to see everyone getting in line for lunch.

"I want to have a group meeting after lunch," he told the group. "So don't leave."

He went over to Bonnie, Hannah and Amanda and asked them to entertain the younger children in the yard after lunch. The girls agreed.

When everyone had finished eating, Mark called the meeting to order. He told everyone about the news reports. He opened the floor for suggestions as to how they should deal with the problems that were mounting.

"I could leave my remote to the fence electrifiers at the computer desk," Brad said. "If anyone shows up at either farm, or if the drones spot people, whoever's at the computer can automatically turn on the electricity to the fences. But they'll need a way to warn the rest of us so no one gets shocked, especially the kids. Actually, we should set up a designated play area and make sure the kids stay in it. That way we know they're safe from the fence and easy to account for in an emergency."

"I think we should use only lanterns at night now," Ginny said. "Just keep the lights off completely. First, it's less of a drain on the generator if it comes on, and it will be less noticeable from the road, especially in the winter when there are no leaves on the trees. Most of us are up with the sun and go to bed soon after the sun sets because we're tired from the day, so it shouldn't be too inconvenient."

"We have solar panels and large marine batteries," Mark said. "Let's start using them to charge electronic devices. Hopefully with hotspots we can still access the news sites.

Adam raised his hand.

"Yes, Adam?" Mark said.

"What if we were to make signs that said the Baptist Church in Elkin has food and put an arrow pointing the way. We could put them at both ends of the road because both of those roads at the intersections go into Elkin. We could take vegetables and venison to the church to help them out. We could even put some signs on the intersections farther out than the ones around us."

"That's a good idea, Adam. I will put you and the other teens in charge of the signs," Mark said. "Keep thinking, everybody." The meeting adjourned.

Tina went outside. She noticed Bonnie and Hannah talking with Amanda, and Amanda was crying. She walked over to them.

"Amanda? What's wrong?" Tina asked. She sat beside the girl and put her arm around her.

"Miss, Tina," Amanda said, trying to catch her breath between sobs. "I don't want to go home. It's miserable there. Dad and Aunt Marley work all day in the garden, cooking and cleaning. All Mom and

Uncle Jack do is watch TV and complain. Mom won't work because she said it will ruin her nails."

Amanda looked down. "Miss Tina, I'm ashamed of my mother. I see all the ladies here working and contributing, and my mother just sits and complains. Aunt Marley is worried about Abby because she hides and doesn't speak when we're at home."

Tina looked at Abby. She was playing with the other little girls, but she wasn't smiling like a girl her age should.

"Thank you for telling me, Amanda," Tina said. "I'm not sure what we can do, because your parents are the ones responsible for you. We can't make any changes without their permission, but I'll talk with Ginny, Mark, and Brad to see if we can help in any way."

Tina went back into the house and found Ginny, Mark, Garrett, and Brad still in the dining room.

She went up to them. "I think there is a problem at the Smith house."

"I have no doubt," Mark said, rolling his eyes and shaking his head. He looked at her. "What do you know?"

"I went outside and saw Amanda crying," Tina said. "She doesn't want to go home. Rob and Marley work all day while Sarah and Jack sit and watch TV. She said Abby hides and says nothing the whole time she's there. I think Robbie stays outside with his dad most of the time. I don't want to do anything that would enable Sarah and Jack to remain lazy, but could we maybe let the kids stay over here one or two nights a week?"

"I suppose we could do that," Mark said. "The bed situation is tight."

"I can sleep on the couch in the parlor on those nights," Tina said. "Then Amanda can bunk in the camper with the other girls."

"Abby can have the fourth bunkbed in the upstairs room with the other little girls," Ginny said, "and there's an air mattress that can be put in the basement bunkroom for Robbie."

"Let me talk to Max," Mark said. "He knows Rob. Maybe he can address the problem."

Mark found Max and told him what was going on. Max shook his head in sympathy.

"That's tough," Max said. "It's hard to know what to do, but if it were my kid, I'd want to know. I'll call him. Maybe he and his sister can come here and discuss it, away from Sarah and Jack." Max walked away and made the call. He talked for a while then walked back to Mark. "I'm going to go get Rob and Marley. Can I borrow the golf cart?"

"Sure," Mark said. "Keys should be in the ignition."

Brad was standing in the backyard when Max returned with Rob and Marley. They sat at a picnic table with Amanda who was still crying. Marley started crying, too.

Tina watched from a distance then walked past Brad on her way to her camper.

"What's going on?" Brad asked, gently taking Tina's arm.

"Things are so bad at the Smith house that the children are being severely affected," Tina told him. "Amanda has basically refused to go back. If her parents agree, she can have my bunk in the camper with Bonnie and Hannah. I can sleep on the couch in the parlor."

"You can have my bed," Brad said. "I'll get an air mattress and sleep in there."

"Ah, that's sweet," she said, giving him a small smile, "but we're getting ahead of ourselves. We can't do anything until the Smiths resolve their own problems."

Carson came out of the house, holding his cell phone out toward Brad.

"Brad," he said, "look at this."

Brad saw the feed from the game cameras. At the Smith house, Jack and Sarah were in the driveway loading suitcases into the trunk of one of the cars. Then Jack came out carrying some boxes. Finally, the two of them got into the car and drove away.

"Is this recorded?" Brad asked.

"Yes," Carson said and played it back.

"I'll go get Mark and Max," Brad said, shaking his head. "This is bad."

Carson replayed the video for the two men. They looked at each other and then over at Rob who was still sitting on the picnic table deep in conversation with Amanda.

"I bet their food was in those boxes," Max said. "They may have just left Rob, Marley and the kids with nothing."

Mark walked over to Rob, "Can we see you for a minute?"

Rob nodded and followed Mark to where Max, Brad and Carson were standing.

Mark looked at Carson. "Show him."

Carson replayed the video for Rob. Rob stood staring at the screen for almost a full minute after it stopped playing.

"I knew they were unhappy," Rob said sadly, "but I never dreamed they would do this. They won't be back. They have no idea what the world is like now, and someone will kill them for the little bit of food and gasoline they have in that car. They never believed what Marley and I tried to tell them about how quickly the rest of the country would go downhill. They thought we were being overly cautious by keeping them separated from civilization. I'd better tell Marley. We need to go see if they left us anything."

"If you have nothing, come back," Mark said. "You can join us, and we can all work together. You both have skills that will contribute. We've already discussed sleeping arrangements for the kids. It won't be a problem."

"I appreciate it, Mark," Rob said. "I may have to take you up on that."

Brad went back into the house. Through the kitchen window, he watched Rob break the news to Marley, and they left with Max on the cart. They looked so defeated. He hated to see that. They were good people.

"What's happening?" Tina asked as she walked up next to him.

"While Rob and Marley were here, Jack and Sarah packed up and left," Brad replied. "We think they took all the food with them. Carson has it all on video."

"That's so sad," Tina said. "I guess I'll be moving to the parlor after all."

"Office," Brad said.

"Parlor."

"Office."

"Parlor." They both laughed.

Brad put his arm around Tina and whispered, "Office." Then he let her go and ran out the back door.

"We'll see about that, Mr. Reed," Tina called out to his retreating form.

⬤

Washington, DC

Donald Evans sat in his temporary office at the White House, angry and disgusted. Ever since Jacob Miller had vanished, President Massey had become incapable of making a decision. Now, after the latest bombings, he had ordered the Cabinet, Supreme Court justices, and members of Congress to evacuate to Mount Weather and other safety bunkers scattered along the Blue Ridge Mountains.

Evans clenched his jaw. On his way out, Massey had told him to "keep things running" until it was safe for his return. The President that Evans had supported had just revealed himself to be a coward. The country needed leadership, and the President had abandoned it. At least the Joint Chiefs were still in Washington. Maybe he could work with them to keep the country stable, because they were teetering on the edge of even deeper chaos.

Rubbing his temples, Evans told his assistant to schedule a meeting with the Joint Chiefs and the directors of the FBI, CIA, and Secret Service. They needed a plan to keep the country safe. He only hoped they could work together without hiding behind jurisdictional turf wars. And then, somehow, they would have to get it approved by a President who had fled.

CHAPTER 28

MAY 1

Switzerland

George Thomas and John Rosen sat in the chalet's study reviewing updates from the United States.

"The latest attacks have been quite successful, especially the one in Washington DC," George said, with a chuckle. "One blast destroyed several blocks behind the Rayburn building, and another one hit within a block of the Supreme Court. Evidently, it was too close for comfort because most of the government officials went into hiding. There's no centralized direction for controlling crime in the cities or getting supplies to those areas where everything is running out. Local governments are on their own, and they're struggling because they've depended on the federal government for everything for so long."

"What a pity," John said with a sarcastic smirk. "I'd almost hoped they would give at least a mild show of resistance. The Massey administration is so weak it's practically working in our favor. How soon before the next phase is ready?"

"It's ready," George said, smiling. "You just need to give the order."

"Excellent." John leaned back in his chair. "Except for the terrorist attacks in the U.S., the rest of the world has been quiet for over a week. Everyone, except the countries sharing borders with Russia or China, should be starting to relax. They will lower their vigilance. Let's start the next phase tomorrow. That should put governments worldwide on edge."

"I'll notify the technicians," George said. "It will go into effect in the United States at midnight, Eastern Daylight Savings Time tomorrow night. The rest of the world will be affected simultaneously."

John considered this. "Is everything ready downstairs?"

"Yes," George replied. "You can move anytime."

"Good. Have the staff make those preparations today. I'll inform the rest of The Committee. They'll want to be home by tomorrow."

"Sounds like a plan," George said. "I'll also let the regional managers know. They can handle their areas."

George left the room. As he walked toward his office, his mind drifted back through his life's journey that had led to this time and place. He remembered that first night in the group home, the night he'd met John. It had been John's first night there, too. The two little boys had huddled together, crying quietly in the large room full of metal beds and strangers. He remembered the harassment from the older boys and how he and John learned to survive it.

He remembered the day his elementary school teacher noticed the bruises on his body and reported them to Social Services. The couple in charge of the group home had separated him and John from the older boys, but with cruelty. They had been given soiled mattresses on the floor in the dirty basement. The couple cared more about the monthly checks they received than the children they were supposed to protect.

What that couple never understood was that the basement became a refuge for him, John, and then for several of the other younger children. Many of those children now served in John's organization as regional managers.

John had learned early the arts of management, organization, and manipulation, all born from necessity. George, to his own surprise, discovered he had a talent for math and engineering. Both boys studied hard in school, earned scholarships, and worked their way through college. They started small, kept quiet, and invested wisely. Eventually, they built a consulting firm with a respectable public face, using it to conceal the money laundering that made them rich enough to make this plan a reality. John became the face of the company and its financial strategist. George became the technical and logistical architect behind it.

George settled into his desk chair and began making the necessary encrypted emails to his managers. They would notify the sleeper cells in their areas. None of the managers knew the whole plan, only the instructions they were given. None of the cells knew about each other; they only knew their direct handler. If any of them were caught, the investigations would stall at the lowest level.

When George stepped out of the room, John retrieved his private cell phone. He called his wife, Carol.

"Are you at home?" he asked when she answered.

"Yes, why?"

"It's time," John said. "Keep an eye on the news tomorrow; it should get interesting. Let the kids continue to use their computers and cell phones as service allows, but if you need to reach me, switch to the new system I installed. Stay close to the house. You may not have much time to react if the military leaders break the agreement and use nuclear weapons. Though honestly, I doubt you will be affected by that. Europe and Asia are far more likely to launch missiles toward each other than they are to attack the U.S. We've managed to pull the U.S. out of global interactions without damaging too many natural resources." He paused. "Well, except for Chicago. That place is toast."

"Oh, poor Chicago," Carol said with a sarcastic laugh. "We have such memories from there." Her tone softened. "We miss you. Are you going to be safe?"

"Don't worry about me," he said. "I'll be behind thick concrete walls, sealed doors and forty feet underground. I still wish you had agreed to come here."

"I know," Carol said, "but this way the kids get to keep a normal life as long as possible. At least we live in a rural area. Hopefully people around here won't be affected too badly."

"They shouldn't be, unless someone gets really stupid and detonates nuclear weapons."

"Let's hope that doesn't happen," Carol said. "Everything here is ready. The kids are out horseback riding, avoiding their lessons again. Can we plan on a video call later?"

"Yes," John replied. "Let's do that after dinner. 7:00 your time."

"We'll be here," she answered.

After a few quiet emotional exchanges, the call ended.

John sat back in his chair. Carol had been one of those younger children who had sought refuge in the basement of the group home. He had developed a soft spot for her the first time he saw her, a tiny girl clinging to him in hero worship and crying herself to sleep that first night. He held her through the night, murmuring words of comfort each time she jolted awake in fear. They had survived their hellish childhoods together in that musty basement, clawed their way out of poverty, and built a life that felt secure. The love that had bound them as children never loosened.

Protecting Carol and his children was his first priority. The thousand acres he had bought in a rural area of the United States had been developed into a neighborhood built around horse farms. Beneath the main office of the farm lay the the bunker and supplies that would keep his family safe if everything collapsed.

Andrew Jones and his wife, Tracy, ran the farm. Andrew had been one of the youngest children he and George had protected in the group home. He had paid for Andrew's college education in agriculture and animal science. Andrew would keep Carol and the kids safe.

John looked at his now-silent phone, took a deep breath and allowed himself to relax. The video call would come in the middle of his night, but he didn't care. He couldn't wait to see his family.

North Carolina, USA

Brad came out of the office and went into the kitchen for breakfast. As it turned out, Tina had won the argument because Mark wanted Brad to stay in the office at night to protect the back door while Pete protected the front door. Tina now slept on a full-size rollaway bed in the parlor, and Amanda Smith had moved into the camper with Grace, Bonnie and Hannah.

Abby and Robbie stayed with their parents at the Smith house, but the atmosphere, while sad at the loss of Jack and Sarah, was more positive. Marley brought the children to school every morning and stayed to help with the cooking and the garden. Rob stayed at the house and tended their garden, but he walked over every evening for dinner and escorted the others home before the sun set. Sarah and Jack had left a little food at the house, but not enough to survive.

The days were getting longer and warmer. The cool season plants in the garden were producing well but only minimally supplementing the menus. That part of the garden was small, originally intended only for two people, Brad and Ginny. The fresh produce brought by the families that first day had already been used up, and the group was looking forward to the warm-season vegetables, which were growing well. Brad set out the tomato plants that he had started under the grow light in the laundry room and gave several dozen to Rob Smith.

Wanting a head start on winter preparations, Brad decided to begin cutting firewood. Electricity was already unreliable, and he knew they would need a steady supply as soon as it got colder. He loaded a chainsaw and a small battery powered saw on the trailer behind the four-wheeler. He and Mike collected Adam, Brett, and Michael and headed to the woods. They returned with a large load of wood on the trailer, and the boys split it before stacking it in rows along the wall of the equipment shed that faced away from the house and campers. They were going to need a tremendus amount of wood for the winter, and Brad wanted it safely stored inside of the fence.

Several times a week, the boys hurried to finish their daily chores so they could head out to the woods and gather as much firewood as possible before dinner. Before long they had an impressive pile of wood stretching the entire length of the shed and standing taller than most of them could reach. The boys were proud of themselves, but Brad burst their bubble by saying it wouldn't get them past New Year's if the power went out.

Brad also stored wood on his farm behind the large shed inside the fence. He thought that if the farm got too crowded, he could move his belongings to live in one room of his house.

CHAPTER 29

MAY 3

North Carolina, USA

The house was quiet. Everyone else was asleep when Bennett made his way from his camper to relieve Robert who was on duty at the computer monitor. He had just sat down in the chair when the lamp in the den flicked off and the computer went dark. Before the generator could kick in, the light came back on, and the computer rebooted. Bennett assumed it was a minor disruption in the power grid.

He pulled out his phone and opened a news app, keeping the volume low. He listened to a reporter while keeping his eyes on the computer screens. The commentators were talking nonstop about the widespread, temporary disruption of the grid, but no one had answers about what caused it.

Half an hour later, one of the few remaining sources in Washington discussed the problems inside government and military computer systems. They were communication failures, data leaks, and unexplained outages.

An hour after that, the commentator reported that similar breaches were being reported across the world. No one knew why. No one knew who to blame.

———◆○◆———

Washington, DC

Donald Evans, Secretary of Defense, was awakened shortly after midnight and informed of the security breach in government computer systems. Instantly alert, he called his staff and ordered them to meet in the Situation Room in one hour.

By the time Evans, his staff and the Joint Chiefs reached the White House, his assistant already had coffee brewing and had sent for food from the kitchen. Evans managed to reach the President through a secured landline, but they agreed there would be no computer-based meetings. Having fled the city, the President insisted on keeping his location secret and feared that any online communication could expose him.

Using landlines and secured cell phones, they contacted military bases and key leaders. When the information was compiled, Evans felt his stomach drop. They had been hit with layers of sophisticated spyware. Even NORAD, supposedly untouchable because it was air-gapped, had suffered corrupted files and internal scrambling. Firewalls had been breached. No one could say which systems were still secure. Bad actors inside the government and military had compromised the integrity of their operations.

Taking a calculated risk, Evans called the Israeli ambassador. After a long conversation, the information became even more staggering. A global cyberattack had taken place with one exception. Israel. Because their systems were still secure, they could monitor the entire world. Unfortunately, other nations were beginning to notice this and were starting to blame Israel for the attack.

Evans reassured the Israeli ambassador that he believed Israel had been deliberately spared to draw suspicion toward them and away from the true culprit. But they had no way of knowing who was responsible. The ambassador assured him Israel's priority was identifying the attacker before somone panicked and launched a first-strike missile in a global war.

At 5:00 am, Evans sat at the conference table in the Situation Room. He had spent the last several hours in intense discussion with the Joint Chiefs. A privacy protocol was in place; every computer and piece of security equipment in the room remained dark until cleared.

"How did this happen?" Donald demanded, looking around the table. "Where were our cybersecurity people who were supposed to prevent something like this."

"Sir," his assistant said, "our digital forensics technicians are already working on it. They've traced the earliest breach attempts. The first was in the FBI. Once that system was compromised, the attackers moved to the CIA, Central Government, and finally the Military. NORAD didn't have a data leak. Their systems are scrambled from within, but they're working on it and should be back online soon. Across the government, anything not air-gapped is being attacked. Every time we secure something, it's countered immediately. It's like they have a mirror into the entire network."

"How is that possible?" Evans asked.

"Someone let them in," the assistant replied. "The CIA and FBI are looking for the technicians whose computers were the entry point. They're currently missing. They took family leave two days ago and haven't been reachable since."

"Where are their families?" Evans asked.

"That's the problem," the assistant replied. "The FBI technician doesn't have any. He has a wife listed in his personnel record, but she can't be located. We traced his history back to a group home in Chicago. Sir, it's the same group home that Greg Becker, Jacob

Miller's assistant, is from. They're both missing. The group home is no longer in operation, but the FBI is investigating it and all the former residents. The CIA technician has a set of elderly parents in Florida, but they haven't heard from their daughter in three weeks. She left them a message that she was taking vacation and going on a trip. She told them not to worry, but they're extremely worried now that the CIA has contacted them."

"What is the connection between the two technicians?" Evans asked.

"We don't know, Sir," the assistant answered. "As far as we can tell, there isn't one. But the coincidence is too big. The agencies are still digging."

Evans sat in silence, his chest tightening. Jacob Miller. Greg Becker. Now two technicians. All four could be guilty of treason. And they still had no answers about who sabotaged NORAD. How deep did this plot go? How far was someone willing to go to bring down the United States?

After two more hours of intense discussion, they finalized a plan for secured communication with military bases, commanders, and troops without using computers. Also, more military personnel would be quietly withdrawn from foreign soil and returned to the United States.

At noon, Donald stared at the sandwich on his plate and the phone beside it. He needed to call the President and report the results of the meeting, but he hesitated. As soon as the breach occurred, the President had told him to "look into it and fix it." He was trying. But did he owe a cowardly, incompetent president a detailed summary of the meeting?

Sighing, he picked up the phone and dialed the President's number.

Switzerland

John Rosen and George Thomas stood in the bunker's communications room. They watched the countdown tick to zero, then monitored the screens as their technicians in remote locations around the world entered the codes. The team in Russia targeted computers in Asia. The team in China targeted Russia and Europe. Chaos was the goal.

When the final confirmations came in, John and George turned to the wall of television screens streaming news from across the world.

The first reports were from Asia where select computer systems were down, but neither China nor Russia had issued statements. Soon complaints began emerging from Europe and Eastern Europe. By the time the United States woke, the news outlets were reporting disruptions in key government and military systems.

John yawned with satisfaction, then stood from his chair and stretched. Time for a coffee break.

⸺⸺◆⸺⸺

North Carolina, USA

After lunch, Mark called a group meeting. During the morning, news reports had mentioned breaches in government communication systems. One reporter had asked how the military was handling the situation in light of the recent terrorist attacks, but the government had not offered any clear answers.

The group decided that their daily lives did not depend on the working computers in the government, at least not yet. The meeting adjourned, and everyone went about their work as usual.

Switzerland

It was late, but the day had gone well. John Rosen scrolled through the online news outlets. His contacts in Russia, China, Europe, and the United States had let him know that the computer attacks were successful. Electrical grids and satellites were untouched, giving average citizens uninterrupted access to the news. They watched continuous coverage of the computer breaches and their government's frantic attempts to contain the damage. Industries were worried about their own computer systems and protecting proprietary information. Health care systems worried about protecting patient confidentiality.

One news article caught John's attention. Europe was blaming Russia and China for the computer attacks. Russia was blaming China and Europe. China was blaming the United States and Russia. Iran was blaming Israel. Countries in Africa and South America were stunned and didn't know who to blame.

John smiled. The United States remained silent. They were compromised and unwilling to provoke anyone. His team had deliberately avoided touching Israel's computers. Eventually the whole world would blame Israel.

Most importantly, no one was looking for a lone culprit. No one was blaming him.

CHAPTER 30

MAY 15

North Carolina, USA

Life on the farm had settled into a routine, and the group began to feel a comfortable sense of security. At midday, everyone squeezed around the picnic tables in the backyard, relaxing, and eating sandwiches from leftover chicken. Donna hurried through the back door and shouted from the porch.

"Motorcycles!"

Everyone froze. Then red cups and forks hit the tables. Mark and Pete moved first. Brad followed behind them, his lunch plate forgotten. They ran into the house and crowded around the monitors.

Six motorcycles and two pickup trucks rolled pass the Johnson's place to the south, then continued past the Reed driveway heading north. For a moment, it looked like they were leaving, until they turned around, and came back. They crept along the road and finally turned into the driveway. The grass planted at the entrance had not fooled them for long.

Bennett didn't bother to check the monitors. He ran straight to his truck and moved it to the driveway just inside the fence. Heather and

Leah gathered the children and rushed them to the basement. Ginny, Erica, and Jacque began laying out medical equipment on the dining room table. The others grabbed firearms and took their places at doors and windows. They had planned for this. Everyone knew their role.

Ginny watched the monitors, narrating what she saw. Two motorcycles hit the spikes and blew their tires. The group stopped while three bikers slowly kicked the grass and pulled up rebar and nails. Then, Ginny reported that the vehicles were still near the road, but three men had vanished from the camera feed.

From an upstairs window, Brad spotted them, three men moving through the trees toward the house. He called the information down to Mark. Moments later, the three men stepped out of the trees and continued up the driveway. They walked with a calm, arrogant confidence, as if the farm belonged to them.

Mark pulled the parlor curtains back just enough to watch their approach from the front windows.

Slowly, the three men approached the fence. One of the bikers stepped ahead of the others. His dark, greasy hair reached his shoulders. His jeans were filthy, and his leather vest, worn without a shirt, stretched over his bulging stomach. He surveyed the house for a moment before shouting.

"Hey, you in the house! We need the doc."

Mark and Pete exchanged a look. It was just like the dream, only a month later.

"I was hoping we could avoid this," Mark muttered.

Pete's jaw clenched as his hands tightened on his rifle. He looked at Ginny and shook his head, silently reminding her that in the dream she'd tried to go with them.

"Whatcha want with the doc?" Bennett's voice cracked across the yard, startling the bikers.

"We need the doc," the leader repeated. "We got horse problems. She comes with us and no one gets hurt."

"She's not going with you," Bennett said. "What's the problem? Maybe she can give you some advice."

"No," the man snapped. "The boss told us to bring her."

"You might as well tell us what's wrong with the horses," Bennett said, voice firm. "Let us help you that way, because she's not going with you. She's temporarily retired from making house calls. It's too dangerous."

"The boss wants her to live at our place and take care of the horses and cows."

"I understand that," Bennett answered patiently, "but you seem to have missed the point I already made. She. Is. Not. Going. With. You."

The man sighed and glanced at his companions before looking back. "Come on, man. Our horses have gone lame. They can't walk without limping or just lying down."

Brad slipped down the stairs, ready to keep Ginny from going outside like she tried to do in the dream. He saw the tears in her eyes. She'd heard every word.

Ginny turned to him. "Where are the supplements?"

"In the shed. Do you know what's wrong with them?"

"Yes. Come with me," she said. "It's laminitis. The supplements and instructions will help them heal."

They slipped out the back door and went to the shed.

"I divided everything by animal," Brad said, pointing to a stack of boxes against the wall. He opened one. Ginny grabbed two bottles, and they returned to the house.

At the office computer, Ginny opened a file with instructions for feeding the horses and treating their feet. She printed it, then handed the paper and supplements to Max at the front door.

Outside, the biker eyed Max warily as he approached Bennett. Max spoke quietly, handed over the package, and stepped back.

"Back away from the fence," Bennett said.

The man complied. Bennett pushed the bottles and the paper

through the wire.

"This is from the doc," he said. "This is being given in good faith. We don't want any trouble." Bennett gave the man a pointed look. "I promise you; we make much better friends than we do enemies."

"I'll take this to the boss," the biker said, looking at the items. "He's not going to be happy. He likes getting his way."

"Well, I figure he'll survive," Bennett said calmly, though Brad could hear the sarcasm dripping from his voice. "We didn't have to give you that much, but like I said, it's all in good faith. Treat your horses better."

The man turned around and led the others back down the driveway, their figures fading into the trees. The cameras picked up their movement close to the road where the others had already loaded the ruined motorcycles into the bed of a pickup truck. After a brief conversation, the bikers mounted their remaining bikes and rode off, deliberately carving ruts in Brad's freshly planted grass.

Brad let out a long, controlled breath. Beside him, Pete's shoulders relaxed as he snapped the safety back on his rifle. Pete quietly watched the computer monitors until the last biker disappeared from view.

Brad looked between Ginny and Mark.

"Two things changed," he said. "The timing is later, and this time, we gave them something to help. Maybe that'll be enough to keep them away."

"Maybe," Mark said. "But for how long? What happens when they run out of supplements or something else goes wrong with their animals. I think it's time to prepare."

Before long, the security team along with Brad, Garrett, Robert, Sharon, and Mike had assembled a thorough plan for defense.

CHAPTER 31

MAY 21

North Carolina, USA

The day dawned clear and warm. Ginny stood in her bedroom, freshly showered and wrapped in a robe. It was her wedding day. She nibbled on the breakfast Jacque had brought to her room and watched the men in the backyard arranging furniture for the ceremony. Barbara's voice drifted through the open window as she directed the placement of flowers from the azaleas, dogwoods camelias, and peonies they found around the farm. The yard was slowly transforming into a beautiful outdoor chapel.

Ginny turned to her bed. She removed the robe and stepped into her mother's wedding gown. A tear threatened to spill down and ruin her carefully applied makeup as she realized her mother wasn't there to watch her get married or her father to walk her down the aisle.

"Here," Jacque said gently, handing her a tissue. "You only get one tear today. They wouldn't want you to cry."

"I know," Ginny replied, dabbing at her eyes. "Garrett and I talked it through last night. Mark and Brad understand, too. I'll be fine."

"Time to finish this," Jacque said as she held the flowers for Ginny's hair. Ginny sat while Jacque fastened the floral crown Ginny chose to wear instead of a veil.

Jacque stepped back and grinned. "You look beautiful." She looked out the window and grinned. "Pete's already in place. He looks restless. I think he's ready to get married."

Ginny laughed, leaning to look over Jacque's shoulder. They turned when they heard a knock on the door.

"Ginny?" Mark called. "Ready?"

Jacque opened the door. Mark and Brad stood there, eyes shining as they saw their sister in their mother's wedding gown. They stepped inside and hugged her.

"They would be so proud," Mark said.

The three siblings laughed as Jacque handed them all tissues.

"I'm going down," Jacque said. "Everyone's watching the back door."

Jacque walked down the stairs, through the back door and across the yard to stand beside Garrett, opposite Pete and Max.

Everyone rose when Ginny came out the door, escorted by both Mark and Brad. Brad caught the tears in Pete's eyes and knew their parents would approve.

Garrett gave his usual Sunday lesson, this time on love. Then Pete and Ginny said their vows.

After the ceremony, everyone celebrated with lunch. Erica surprised everyone by revealing a large wedding cake, which disappeared quickly. Then everyone changed out of their best clothes and resumed their usual Sunday routine.

Pete moved out of his room and into Ginny's. Bennett moved from the camper to Pete's room to guard the front door. Jacque and Melanie, who had been staying in Ginny's room, moved into the camper Bennett vacated.

The only one confused about the changing arrangements was two-year-old Jackson.

After lunch, Brad approached Tina, who was washing dishes. "I'm going to walk to the farmhouse. Would you like to go?"

Tina gave him a big smile. "Yes, I would."

Brad led her down a path she had not traveled before. They walked between two corn fields before entering the woods and approaching his pond. The world was quiet except for the wind and their conversation. Tina stopped, bent over and examined the rocks under their feet.

"What are you looking for?" Brad asked.

"These," she said as she picked up several carefully selected specimens. She flung the first rock out over the water. They watched it skip over the smooth surface of the pond and create ripples in its wake.

Accepting the challenge, Brad searched for his own handful of rocks. They spent several minutes skimming rocks across the surface, and Tina told him she wanted to come back and go fishing sometime.

"Soon," she urged as they started moving toward Brad's house again.

Before long she could make out the barn and equipment shed through the trees. She smiled. She loved coming to this house. It had been a place of peace and joy in her dream, and she felt that way whenever she was here. Even though there was very little inside, walking up to the almost-empty house felt like coming home. Brad unlocked the gate, held it open for her, then refastened the lock behind her. He unlocked the screen door, and they went onto the back porch.

"I love this porch," Tina said. "It's speaks of labor and love. I can just see that table full of vegetables to be sorted and prepared for canning. I can see myself sitting in that rocking chair breaking green beans or peeling fruit for jelly."

"You can?" Brad asked.

"Yes," Tina answered. "I saw it in my dream. I loved it here."

"Even though it's primitive compared to Ginny's house or even the

Smith house?" Brad asked, looking at the vintage appliances and scuff marks on the hardwood floors.

"Yes. Even then," Tina said. "Oh sure, it needs a good cleaning and some love, but I can live without central heat and air. I grew up that way. I know what it's like."

"I had you pictured as a soft, city girl," Brad chuckled. "I never guessed you would be a hardy, hardworking country girl."

Tina giggled. "I'm stronger than I look."

They went into the kitchen. Cabinets lined the outside wall of the room that housed the sink. She opened one. There were some large, older bowls and pie plates left.

"I guess they didn't want these," Tina said, taking one down that had a matching lid. "It's not bad. It would hold a casserole." In another cabinet she found neat stacks of glasses, cups, and a set of dishes.

"My grandmother had a set like this," she said. "Her mother got them with trading stamps back in the 1950s." Tina crouched and opened a door in a lower cabinet.

"Oh, look! They left a set of cast iron skillets and some pots!" Tina looked around at him, excitement shining in her face. "Brad, they left you enough to set up housekeeping."

Tina walked into the dining room. There was one chair by a window. Across the hall in the parlor was a matching chair. Tina giggled and moved them both to the small table in the kitchen.

"See!" she said, "a table for two."

Tina went back into the parlor where the Thompsons had left two matching recliners, a table and a lamp. Tina sat in one.

"They work, Brad," she said. "They just need some upholstery cleaning."

Tina found a set of sheets, a bed spread, some towels, wash cloths and bathroom rugs in the cabinets in the downstairs bathroom, but what excited her was finding the kitchen towels, cloths, and aprons. She unfolded everything and found they were in good shape, not threadbare or torn.

When they went upstairs, one bedroom had an antique bed with a high headboard and a dresser to match. The largest bedroom had no furniture. There were linens in the upstairs bathroom closet, and an empty cedar chest had been left in the third bedroom. Brad checked the flues. Every fireplace had an open, working chimney.

"Brad, where's the garden plot for this house?" she asked.

"There's a small one inside the fence behind the barn," he said. "There's also a larger one beside the house outside the fence."

"We should go ahead and plant the one behind the barn. There are game cameras here. If someone tries to steal the food, you can be down here before they leave." She paused and looked at Brad. "Let's check the pantry."

Tina almost ran down the stairs and into the pantry. She opened a cabinet door and saw what she wanted.

"Look!" she exclaimed. "Canning jars!" In another cabinet she found the canner and boxes of jar lids.

She looked through the boxes of lids. "Oh, bless that woman's heart. She has some of the reusable lids with rubber rings."

"Brad," Tina said, looking him with excitement. "You could move in here if you want. It's doable."

Brad walked over to Tina, bent down and kissed her. It was not a gentle, probing kiss, but it wasn't rushed, either. It was the kiss of a man who knew exactly what he wanted.

Tina kissed him back. She put her arms around his neck and kissed him with all the emotion she had suppressed since she had seen him in her dream. To her the kiss was familiar, safe, and arousing. To Brad it was new, exciting, and he had never felt like this with any other woman, not even Holly.

"You said I was in your dream," Brad said quietly, breaking away enough to look her in the eyes.

"Umhmm," answered Tina, gripping his shoulders while his arms still wrapped around her waist.

"Was I in your dream like this?" he asked.

"Yes," Tina answered.

"We kissed?"

"Yes," Tina answered, giving him a mischievous grin.

"Were we here?" he asked.

"Yes."

He was quiet for a moment, his eyes studying her face, looking for answers to his questions.

"Were we married?" he asked, watching her closely.

Tina hesitated then quietly said, "Yes." She took a deep breath, broke the embrace and calmly looked at Brad. "But that does not mean you are required to marry me." Her heart was beating rapidly, hoping she didn't change how Brad saw her. "We have proven the dreams can change."

"You feel you know me because we had already met and married in your dream," Brad said. "I'm just getting to know you, but I like the idea."

Brad took her hand and led her to one of the chairs in the kitchen. He sat in the other, and they talked about the house, the farm, and possibilities.

"Will Ginny let me have some cleaning supplies?" Tina asked. "I could come over after classes and start cleaning and getting things ready for you to move in if you ever want to. I would suggest some mouse traps, though. I saw evidence in the pantry."

Brad pulled Tina out of her chair and toward him until she fell onto his lap. He wanted her closer. She put her arm around his neck and absently played with the curls on the back of his neck. He absently stroked her back. They stayed that way for hours, talking quietly about their hopes and dreams. About who they had been and who they hoped to become.

When the room started to grow dark, Brad said, "We had better get back. It's past dinner." They left the house and walked back to Ginny's.

Ginny stood in the backyard cleaning the picnic tables after dinner when she saw Brad and Tina walking back to the house holding hands.

She tapped Garrett on the shoulder and said, "Look." She pointed to the couple walking toward them. She smiled when she saw their clasped hands swinging slightly as they laughed quietly together.

"I wondered how long that would take," Garrett said. "I think she's God's replacement for Holly, and I believe she's better for him than Holly ever would have been."

"I agree," said Ginny.

As they approached the house Brad said, "I have one more question. When did you say you had the dream?"

"April 7th," Tina answered. "I will never forget that date. Why?"

"I just wondered."

Brad realized that April 7 was two days after Holly had broken up with him. That was the change, the complete disruption of the dream and reality, that allowed Tina to be included in this group. Brad felt the weight of it settle over him, not heavy, just humbling.

He said a silent prayer of thanks. Not for Holly's leaving, though now he could see the mercy in it. Not for the dream, though it had guided them more than once. But for Tina, for the way she fit into his life with quiet inevitability, as though she was always meant to be there.

These feelings were developing fast. He should be wary, but he wasn't. It felt right, like a gift, like his life had suddenly gotten on the track it was always supposed to be on.

CHAPTER 32

MAY 22

Switzerland

The second phase of the computer attacks was set in motion. Some of the countries had been able to rebuild secure communication systems for their government and military, but they weren't prepared for the assault that followed, one aimed at mass transit systems, airports and electrical grids.

Reports began filtering in. Subway trains grinding to a halt while filled with people who were then stranded in dark tunnels; stoplights in major cities going dark; draw bridges freezing in mid-lift, leaving motorists stuck on the spans and ships unable to move. Flights across the globe were cancelled, not just in the United States. Then the power failures began. Electricity in selected large cities all over the world went out, leaving citizens without lights, refrigeration or fresh running water.

John Rosen smiled. Now the average citizen would be affected. Outages would cause increased levels of crime in countries around the world, including in the United States. Telecommunications and media companies were left untouched, for now. He needed them active, broadcasting fear, amplifying chaos, and informing the world of the threats and problems happening everywhere.

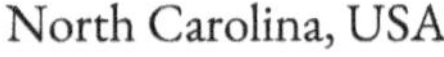

North Carolina, USA

Before breakfast, Tina asked Ginny if she could use some cleaning supplies. She and Brad were going to try to get his house livable since there seemed to be more people in the group. She and Ginny both believed the remnants of the Smith family would eventually move into the compound.

Ginny smiled and told Tina to use what she needed.

Brad came into the kitchen for breakfast. Once again people clustered around the television. What now. He thought about ignoring it, but his curiosity won. He walked over to see what had everyone's attention.

The only television station still broadcasting consistently was the one in Winston-Salem. Brad usually listened without watching, so the sight on the screen startled him. The normally polished news anchor looked exhausted. Her hair was pulled back instead of professionanlly styled, her clothes were wrinkled, and her face was so gaunt that Brad wondered when her last meal had been. She reported that goverment and military computer systems were still compromised, and now, mass transportation systems and portions of the electrical grid were malfunctioning as well.

Then, as if to make a point, the power went out.

Brad shook his head. He unplugged unnecessary items in the office and left the group. He had a garden to prepare on his farm.

While Tina taught classes, Brad plowed and smoothed the garden plot. At noon, Brad went back to the house for lunch. After lunch, Tina returned to the house with him and helped him plant tomatoes, green beans, squash, cucumbers, lima beans, cantaloupe and watermelons.

When they finished in the garden, Tina followed Brad into the house, and together they started cleaning the kitchen. Before going back to the main house, they collected all the linens to be washed. They laughed about the possibility of washing everything by hand if the power had not returned.

Neither of them said it aloud, but both felt they were getting the house ready to be their home after they got married.

CHAPTER 33

MAY 25

Brad and Tina were working at the house. Their garden was planted. The kitchen and dishes had been cleaned, and Tina was working in the upstairs bathroom. When she was finished, she started down the stairs. Brad met her at the bottom. She was standing two steps above him which brought her face equal with his.

She wrapped her arms around him and pulled him close. Then she kissed him.

"I like being at your height. Kissing is very easy."

Brad laughed. "We can get you some stilts. That way you can kiss me and reach the top shelf in the cabinets."

"I don't need a top shelf," she teased. "We don't have enough to fill the cabinets up that high."

"You said we. Is that how you feel?" Brad asked.

"Yes. I think of us as a 'we.' I've thought of us as a 'we' for a lot longer than you know."

"Me too," Brad said, softly. "So, Tina, will you become a 'we' with me. Will you marry me?"

"Yes," Tina said, closing her eyes. She stepped down one stair and leaned into him, her face now buried in his chest. "I thought you would never ask. I was afraid the man of my dreams had decided on a different dream."

"That will never happen," Brad said as he dropped his head toward hers. His cheek rested on the top of her head, and he breathed in the scent of her shampoo. "When do you want to do this?"

"Is Sunday too soon?" she asked.

"Are you sure?" Brad laughed, leaning back to look at her. "Sounds like you're afraid I'll get away."

"Yes, I'm sure," Tina said confidently, her arms still looped around Brad's neck. "And I'm not worried about your getting away." She grinned. "You'd be crazy to give up a pioneer woman like me."

Brad burst into laughter. "You're right about that."

We have a kitchen and a bathroom," Tina said. "By Sunday I'll have the bedroom clean and sheets on the bed. But we may want to rethink it. It's too short for you."

"Hmm. You're right," he said, remembering the size of the antique bed upstairs. "Let me think about this."

That evening, everyone ate dinner outside on the picnic tables, enjoying the cooler evening breeze. Brad stood and cleared his throat to get everyone's attention.

"I have an announcement," he said, gently pulling Tina to her feet to stand beside him. "I know this may be unexpected, but this afternoon I asked Tina to marry me. I still can't believe it, but she said yes."

The group erupted in clapping, cheers, and whistles.

"When's the date?" Ginny asked, running up to hug them both.

"A week from Sunday," Brad said. "We still have to get the house ready."

"So, you're moving in over there?" Mark asked.

"Yes," Brad answered. "We want to use that house, and it'll free up the office for someone here."

"Won't it be gloomy there with the windows and doors boarded up?" Barbara asked.

"I found shutters in the barn for the windows," Brad said. "We'll leave the plywood over the front door, but I'll put up the shutters over the windows. We'll need the light and cross breeze since there's no air conditioning."

"Do you have any furniture?" Leah asked.

"Some," Tina said. "We have a kitchen table, two chairs, a few dishes, skillets, and two recliners left in the parlor. There is one bed and a matching dresser upstairs. That's it." She laughed.

Ginny glanced at Leah. Her cheeks were red, and her jaw was tight. Ginny thought the woman looked nervous. It took her a moment before she realized why. Leah was afraid Brad would want his bedroom suit back, the one Leah had been sleeping on since coming to the farm.

Annoyance flared hot in Ginny's chest. The furniture was Brad's. If he wanted it, he should have it. While everyone was talking at once, asking Tina and Brad questions, Ginny moved over to Garrett. She leaned toward him and got his attention before she quietly spoke.

"Brad owns the bedroom suit where Robert and Leah are staying," she said. "Notice how nervous Leah looks? She's afraid Brad will want it, but it belongs to him. Shouldn't he be able to take it?"

Garrett looked at Leah.

He sighed. "You're right, of course, but what will the Dickson's do?"

Ginny felt heat rush to her cheeks.

"Brad gave up his room for them," she said quietly, but not hiding her anger. "Are you saying he should give up his belongings too? They could have brought furniture. As far as I'm concerned, they can go out to a camper or sleep on an air mattress."

"Calm down," Garrett said calmly, dropping a hand on her shoulder and pulling her away from the others. "Let me talk to Brad. He may already have a plan. Let's not jump to conclusions."

"He's your brother, and they are your friends," Ginny said. "You're the one who can sort this out. Brad has already done a lot for them. All of us have. He spent most of his money on the fencing to keep us safe along with seeds, fertilizer and lime to keep us in food. What have the Dickson's brought? Nothing but themselves and the things that they just did not want to leave behind. Michael contributed more with his fruit trees than his parents have. All I'm saying is, don't let them take advantage of Brad." She paused, took a deep breath and gave Garrett a pointed look. "If you don't handle it, I will, and I won't be nearly as diplomatic as you are."

Ginny walked away toward the barn. She needed to calm down and walking always helped.

Pete joined her.

"You're upset," he said. "What's going on?"

"Did you see the look on Leah's face when Brad announced his engagement?" Ginny asked. "She's terrified he'll want his bedroom suit. He bought it, so it belongs to him. He should take it. They can sleep on an air mattress until we can figure out how to replace it. They brought nothing but themselves, their clothing, and some food, which is long gone. Brad spent most of his savings on this fence that is keeping us safe, and the supplies to grow food."

"I agree," he said calmly, "but I think you're borrowing trouble. Let Brad and Tina work this out. They might not even need it."

"I know, Ginny said, rubbing her temples. "But I saw her face, and I knew exactly what she was thinking. It made me mad."

Pete guided Ginny to the back corner of the barn and pulled her into his arms. He tucked her head beneath his chin and squeezed her tight.

"I know," he murmured into her hair. "I agree with you, but we can't do anything about it. We can't control this. We're all living in close quarters. It's not worth starting a fight we don't need. This is between Brad and them."

"You're right," Ginny sighed. "That's why I am out here walking off my mad."

Pete laughed and suggested another activity for relieving stress.

She laughed and playfully pushed him away. She strolled a few paces toward the house before turning back to smirk at him. "Later."

• • •

Washington, DC

Donald Evans yawned and rubbed his eyes. He was exhausted. He needed a shower, a change of clothes, and a decent meal. But for the first time in days, he felt a small glimmer of hope. After a marathon of meetings with the Joint Chiefs and the heads of the CIA, FBI, and Secret Service, the day had been surprisingly productive.

A handful of enterprising technicians had managed to keep their private computers secure. Using their own encryption systems, the agencies had quietly built a new secure network for the government and CIA. The FBI and Secret Service would be restored in a few days. However, the mass transit and infrastructure systems were still struggling to come back online.

Evans also learned that the cyberattacks were being traced through servers around the world. Every attempt to trace it back to a single culprit was blocked at different points. The only thing nations could agree on was that whoever had launched the global attacks had hidden their identity with amazing skill.

One development stood out. A CIA operative in Europe had reported an unusual concentration of wealthy and influential individuals in Switzerland, enough to draw attention. That alone wasn't suspicious. What caught the CIA's attention was the mass exodus of this group from Switzerland one day before the computer attack. The operative had sent a list of the names to Washington. High ranking government officials from China, Russia, South Africa, and Brazil had been there, the same countries that had supplied explosives for the terrorist attacks.

Evans had kept an open communication with the ambassador from Israel, but he hadn't shared this news. Israel might have the same information, but it was to the United States' advantage to appear as blindsighted and overwhelmed as everyone else.

Another piece of news made Evans smile. The Secret Service and CIA had both opened investigations into Jacob Miller. They had managed to trace his disappearance to Belize, where he had recently bought property under a false name. The investigations had unearthed large amounts of money being deposited into a Swiss bank account filed under the same alias. The money came from what appeared to be a shell corporation. The forensic accountants were still trying to untangle the layers of ownership, but the trail was deliberately and expertly obscured.

Evans looked at his watch. A CIA operative in South America would be paying Jacob Miller a visit tonight. He couldn't wait to hear the result of that meeting.

⸺◦⸺

Switzerland

John stood in the communications center watching the monitors. He could see, in real time, the world scrambling to identify who was responsible for the cascading computer problems. George walked up beside him.

"Our firewalls are holding," he reported. "They got past the first one, but we planned on making that one easy for them, to give them a false sense of progress. The rest should hold. And even if someone breaks through another layer, it will point them to servers in both China and Russia. Our people there were thorough and have already left those countries."

"Good," John said. "How are our people in the U.S.? Are they angry that they weren't included in this phase?"

"Yes," George admitted, "but they also understand the benefit of plausible deniability. They can't be blamed for it, which means they will still be in place when we return to the U.S."

He paused. "The U.S. Government found Jacob Miller. They also found his Swiss bank account, but they've been unable to trace the money back to us. Yet."

"Yet?" John asked.

"My source tells me a CIA operative should be visiting Miller sometime this evening, Belize time."

"We'd better get to him first," John said.

"Already taking care of that," George said. "Jacob will have the choice to either leave alive with our people, or be found dead by the CIA."

"We probably shouldn't give him a choice," John said. "He's weak." John looked at George. "He'll probably write a suicide note expressing his regret for treason and working with China."

George nodded, took out his phone and left the bunker.

CHAPTER 34

MAY 25

Washington DC

Donald Evans paced the halls between the offices of the West Wing. "Are you sure?" he asked his assistant, stopping to look at the man.

"Yes, Sir," the young man replied. "Jacob Miller's body was found this morning by his housekeeper. A suicide note was beside him. He admitted to treason and to working with China to coordinate the terrorist attacks against the United States."

"Call another meeting of the core group from yesterday," Donald said. "I want to know exactly what the CIA found when they arrived. What about his aide? In the meeting they mentioned that he had also left the country."

"Greg Becker is unaccounted for," the assistant admitted.

The leaders of the military and security agencies of the United States took sandwiches, chips, and drinks from a side table before they gathered around the large table that dominated the Situation Room, which had been cleared of the old security and computer systems. No one would be able to listen in on this meeting.

Donald Evans listened intently as the Director of the CIA described the scene at the Miller estate in Belize. Mrs. Miller was shocked and horrified at what the death of her husband implied. Donald believed her declaration that she had no idea that her husband had been working with a foreign entity against the United States. She understood that Miller's assets would be frozen until the investigation could separate their legitimate income from what appeared to be payments for his work against the government, and she was grateful to be allowed to stay at the Belize estate with her daughter.

"Was it really suicide?" Donald finally asked.

"The official report is suicide," the CIA director reported. "However, we highly doubt it. We think he was killed before he could agree to give us information in a plea bargain."

"His note said he was working with China," Donald said. "Can we trace his deposits to that government?"

"Not yet," was the answer from the CIA director. "Even if we do, I'm not completely sure I believe that. Trace evidence from the terrorist bombs are from multiple countries. Someone wants us to believe China is responsible."

"Where's Greg Becker?" Evans asked.

"We're still looking," the FBI director said. "We traced both of their movements to Miami. Miller went from there to Nassau then to Belize. Becker disappeared in Miami. His bank accounts were closed the day they disappeared, and his credit cards have been inactive. He has no immediate family; he was raised in a foster home in Chicago. It's like he's a ghost."

⸺◆⸺

Miami, Florida, USA

"How are you feeling?"

Greg Becker opened his eyes to see his best friend, Kaylin. He smiled.

"Getting better, thank you," he answered quietly as he took her hand. "Couldn't have done this without you."

Kaylin smiled, "I'm glad you told me to leave Chicago when you did. Miami is a lot better, even with the bombs." She looked at his face. "The bruises are fading, but I still can't get used to this new look."

Greg laughed then grimaced, "Don't make me smile too big. The incisions over the chin and nose are still sore. I'll be glad when I can wear glasses."

"No worries," she said. "That time will be here before you know it. Roger says as soon as you can stand to wear makeup, we'll get a new passport made for you."

Roger was the territory manager for the company both she and Greg worked for. Roger was fifteen years older than they were, and had grown up in the same Chicago group home.

"Do we have a new assignment?" Greg asked.

"Not until you're well and have established a new identity," Kaylin answered. "I think we'll be a couple and assigned temporarily to another country."

"I like that," Greg smiled, closing his eyes. "A couple."

"Me too," she replied softly, still holding his hand.

CHAPTER 35

JUNE 4

Switzerland

John Rosen stood in the communications area of his bunker while the last phase of the cyber attack was taking place. He smiled. Only he, George, and the technicians knew about this one. The Committee didn't know. The participating countries didn't know.

This would be the biggest blow to the world. Every government, military, and private company with a satellite in orbit would think it had suffered a minor glitch, a blip, a blink, before everything appeared normal again. During that blink, he had one team jamming the uplink while another team slipped in a forged command packet. Then the data would be flowing to him.

Eventually, governments and companies would realize that while their satellites were orbiting, no information was being relayed to the appropriate servers. The satellite owners would scramble, trying to figure out the problem. During that time, he alone would be able to tell what everyone in the world was doing, what the weather was doing, and most importantly, what armies were doing.

The chaos from this would be beautiful. GPS programs would

degrade or fail. John chuckled; he hoped there were enough road maps to fill the gap until the GPS was back online. Air traffic controllers would scramble to coordinate plane positions with radio communications and ground radar. NOAA would lose the ability to predict the weather. And governments couldn't spy on their enemies.

But nothing would last forever. Governments, agencies, and private companies would regain control of their computers and satellites. Jamming software would become ineffective, and life would return to a relative normal. Almost.

A sweet form of suspicion would exist. Europe would blame the BRICS nations. The BRICS block would blame Europe, and it members would blame each other. New alliances would falter, and old grudges would resurface.

Then, when the anger and shouting reached its peak, he would insert himself as the mediator, the calm voice, a man of reason. He would become the man the world didn't know it needed.

He chuckled; he had left Israel's satellites alone. If this doesn't make someone attack Israel, then he didn't know what would. He almost felt bad for Israel. He didn't have anything against the country. He just needed attention focused somewhere besides on Switzerland and him.

⸻◆⸻

Washington, DC

Donald Evans inhaled sharply as his pulse rate ticked up a notch. The latest report showed a quick blip in the transmissions from their military satellites. It was suspicious enough that technicians across the military sprang into action.

It didn't take long to find out that data being transmitted from the satellites was being hijacked. Fortunately, in this case, they were able to tell that the data was being downloaded in both Russia and China.

Then it was being relayed through servers to a final destination which hadn't been identified yet. Maybe, just maybe, they'd finally trace the relays back to whoever was responsible for the attacks on the United States.

⸺◦⸺

North Carolina, USA

The anticipated Sunday morning was clear and warm. Once again, the backyard had been transformed into a chapel. Chairs were arranged for watching the ceremony, and flowers covered a makeshift arbor in front of the crowd.

In Ginny's room, Tina put on the white dress she bought in a boutique after she had her dream. Ginny and Jacque fixed her hair and makeup, while Tina tried and failed to control the smile etching across her face.

"Do you see Brad?" she asked. "Is he in the backyard?"

Ginny looked out the window. "He's there, looking nervous but smiling like an idiot."

Tina laughed. "How do I look?"

"Like a beautiful bride," Jacque answered. "Let's go downstairs. Aaron is waiting to escort you down the aisle."

Tina carefully walked down the stairs, mindful of the flowers in her hair. She smiled at Aaron. The two had grown close during the last two months. He treated her like a family member, and she cherished that.

Brad's eyes glazed with tears as he watched his bride walk toward him. They turned to Garrett who gave another lesson on love and joined Brad and Tina in matrimony.

When the service was over, Tina was beaming. She had someone snap a picture of her and Brad with Brad's phone. She sent it to her parents who knew this was her wedding day. They called her back, telling her how beautiful she was, how they wished they could be there, and how much they were looking forward to meeting Brad.

The wedding was followed by lunch and wedding cake. The Smiths and the Suttons came for the celebration, just as they had for Ginny's wedding. While he was at the farm, Jerry Sutton asked Garrett if he would marry him and his girlfriend. Again, the group erupted in loud clapping and cheers. It felt good to have something to celebrate.

After lunch, Tina changed clothes and started to pack her few belongings into her suitcases and bins. She was so excited. She could hardly believe she was going to be a wife in her own home. She had just zipped her suitcase closed when she heard Brett's voice tear through the den, frantic, panicked, and terrified. He was shouting that the large group of motorcycles was coming back.

As arranged, Leah, Ceely, Marley and Tina gathered the children and teenagers in Brad's and Mark's trucks. They slipped out the gate behind the shed. Tina and Ceely drove as fast as they dared down the farm paths to the barn behind Brad's house. They unloaded as quickly as they could and slipped quietly into the house.

Tina gathered the group in the kitchen so they would be close to the cellar if they needed to hide. Brad and Mike had built a door over the stairwell to the basement that looked like a storage cabinet; it was just another layer of safety. Then she and Ceely went upstairs to keep watch from the windows. All they could do now was wait.

When the alarm for the motorcycles had gone out, the adults dropped what they were doing. They ran to their prearranged positions, picking up the rifle or shotgun that had been hung there well out of reach of the children. The driveway had defensive measures in place. They waited.

On the monitor they could see the motorcycle gang stop at the end of the driveway. It was larger than the previous group that had received the supplements. Two men got off their bikes and walked ahead, pulling up the rebar and nails as they went. Once the road was clear, the group rode forward and stopped at the fence.

A man they had not seen before got off his bike. He was taller than the first biker who had demanded Ginny. His hair and beard were cleaner, trimmed, and he wore a black t-shirt that stretched over his bulging abdomen.

"We need the doc," he yelled. "Give us the doc and no one gets hurt."

This time Bennett was not at the fence. He stood behind the bulletproof door of his truck, parked back from the fence but with a clear view of the driveway. Mark, who was stationed at the parlor windows, answered through a bullhorn.

"We gave you treatment and instructions," Mark said. "Why do you still need her? We already told you, Doc doesn't make house calls anymore."

"We did what she said," the man called back. "The horses got better then they got bad again. Something's wrong. We need the horses, and we need the doc."

"Well, I'm sorry about your horses," Mark called out, "but the doc isn't going with you. You'll have to figure it out yourself."

The leader calmly shook his head, almost pityingly, as if the people in the house were too dense to understand. He motioned for his men to get closer to the fence.

Everyone in the house tensed. The sound of gun safeties being switched off could be heard echoing through the rooms; it was a chorus of ominous clicks.

"This is your last warning," the leader yelled.

Mark started to answer when Sharon came up behind him, her face tight with fury.

She held out her hand and said, "Give me that bullhorn."

Startled, Mark handed it to her.

She snatched it and bellowed, "Roy Lee Ingram, what the hell do you think you're doing, terrorizing innocent, peace-loving people?"

Mark burst into laughter before clamping it down.

"Roy Lee?" he whispered.

Sharon rolled her eyes. "My stupid brother. I had no idea where he was until I looked out the window and saw the idiot acting all brave. He was always a blowhard who thought more of himself than anyone else did."

The leader paused and looked shocked. The men at the windows in the house could see the bikers behind the leader snicker into their hands.

"Sharon? Is that you?" the leader asked loudly. "You get out here with me where you're safe, and my name is Boss."

Sharon shoved the bullhorn back into Mark's hands. "His name is idiot. No, make that lazy idiot. I'm going out on the porch. He won't let anyone hurt me. I may think he's useless, but he's still my brother, and I always took up for him outside the family."

Sharon walked out onto the porch with her hands raised, moving slowly. She placed her rifle on the chair beside her, straightened her shoulders and stood facing her brother.

"Okay Boss," she said, drawing out the name with thick sarcasm. "Tell me about your horses."

"They're lame," he answered. "They can't pull a plow."

"Are you feeding them?" she asked.

"Well, yeah," he answered.

"Is there anyone back at wherever you live that could take a picture of the horses and their hooves and send it to you?" she asked.

"Yeah, I'll call 'em." Boss turned back to his men. "Have a seat and rest. This could take a while, and I need you to be ready at any moment, not tired." Boss made the phone call.

A few minutes later, he shouted to Sharon. "I got someone doing that. It may take a while."

"I'm in no rush," Sharon said.

Ten minutes later Boss shouted, "Sharon, I got the pictures."

"Good. Send them to me," she called back to him. "Do you still have the number? It hasn't changed."

"Yeah. I got it. Here they come."

"I'm going inside to show them to the doc," Sharon said loudly. "Don't do anything stupid, Boss. There are armed men watching you. I don't want to lose a brother today."

Sharon went inside where Ginny was waiting. Ginny looked at the pictures, and tears rolled down her cheeks.

"Oh, those poor animals," she said. Ginny thought for a moment. "Sharon, ask him if he as any horse trailers."

Sharon went out on the porch and called, "Do y'all have any horse trailers where you're staying?"

"We got a few," he answered.

Ginny came up behind the door and said, "Ask him if he would bring the sickest of the animals here. I will treat them and get them healthy again."

Sharon relayed the message.

"I can only bring four," Boss said. "What about the rest?"

"Well, Boss," Sharon said dripping sarcasm, "try making several trips."

Ginny added, "Ask if he has anyone that he could send for me to teach how to care for the horses, so this doesn't happen again."

Sharon relayed the message.

"Yeah. I can do that," Boss answered.

"Well then, you better go," Sharon said. "You can get the first set of trailers loaded and here before dark."

"Okay," Boss said. "We'll try this first."

"Don't be foolish, Boss," Sharon said. "We're extending the hand of friendship. No, make that the helping hand. Try building alliances and not killing people to get your own way. That's the way the special forces do it, Boss. Be like them."

Sharon watched his brother stand tall, puffing with pride.

"Good idea, Sharon," he said. "We'll be back with the horses." Boss turned to his gang. "Mount up, boys. We're playing special forces today."

One of the men mumbled and Boss smacked him over the head.

"Not here, and I mean it," he snapped. "No one harms the women here, you got me?"

When Sharon heard it, her blood ran cold. What had her brother gotten tangled up in.

Mark watched the motorcyclists leave. When he could no longer hear their motors he called out, "It's over. Stand down."

Sharon stepped back inside, and Ginny wapped her in a tight hug.

"You saved Pete's life today," Ginny said.

Sharon had tears in her eyes.

"No," she said. "Pete would have been fine. If anything, I saved my brother's life today. That group couldn't survive what we have hidden along the drive or what's waiting inside the fence."

"Good work, Sharon," Brad said as he came up beside them. "Thank you."

Brad turned to his sister.

"Ginny, Robert and I are going to take your truck and tell the others they can come back."

"Keys are in the glove box," she said.

At his farm, Brad parked behind the barn beside the other trucks. He and Robert got out and walked around to the fence.

He unlocked the gate and called, "Tina. We're coming in."

Brad locked the fence behind them, turned and saw Tina sprinting out of the house. She launched herself into his arms.

"I was so scared I would become a widow on my wedding day," she said and cried briefly with joy.

Brad held her tight.

"It's all right," he said. "There was no fight. I'll tell you the whole story when everyone's gone."

Robert and Ceely loaded the women and children in Mark's and Ginny's trucks. When everyone was gone, Brad and Tina sat at the kitchen table.

"Tell me what happened!" Tina said. "I'm dying to know."

Brad repeated the entire exchange between Sharon and her brother.

Tina burst out laughing. "Roy Lee? That's so southern, but I agree, Boss sounds more ominous. I'm glad we had a peaceful solution. It's amazing that Max and Sharon weren't in your dream, but they're here now, and we know exactly why God put them here."

Tina paused. "I have one more question."

"Yes?"

"Where did you get that beautiful king-sized bed and the linens to fit it?" she asked.

Brad smiled. "I have a friend, Eric, in Elkin who conveniently works for a furniture store. I traded two dozen eggs, a case of coffee, and a case of my sodas for that bed. He was so glad he told me to come back for furniture anytime. While you were teaching, Mark, Pete, and Garrett went with me to Elkin to get it."

His expession dimmed. "Elkin is like a ghost town. No one goes downtown because there's nothing left. Anything of value has been looted. Eric's store is north of town and luckily hadn't been vandalized. Furniture hasn't been a high priority for looters, yet. He said the Larkin gang was killed by vigilantes in Elkin who got tired of their stealing and brutalizing people. They were the ones who did most of the looting. The people of Elkin are really good people. They'll work together and come out at the end of this stronger.

Tina stood and said, "Well, I think we should try out the bed that friend sold you. I can't believe you gave up a case of your sodas."

Brad wriggled his eyebrows. "For you and that bed, I would have given him two."

Bennett left his truck and walked through the back door of the house and into the kitchen. Jacque and Ginny were quietly putting away medical supplies, but what caught his attention was Pete's expression. He was leaning against the wall in the dining room, frowning as he watched Ginny.

Bennett walked over. "You all right?"

Pete pursed his lips and shook his head. "We know they're coming back. What we don't know is if they're bringing horses or reinforcements."

"You're right," Bennett said. He caught the attention of Mark, Alex, and Max and motioned them over.

When the five men were in a huddle, Bennett said, "They're coming back. Pete's right. We don't know what they're bringing. We need to be prepared."

The men went into the parlor and began the process of getting prepared to win a war with the motorcycle gang that was coming back.

Look for *Taking a Chance*, Book 3 in the Forewarned Series. Dr. Jacque Meyers waited until the day chaos erupted to try to get to the farm. Now, she and her daughter, Melanie Barefoot, are having to navigate congested roads, refugees, and medical emergencies in the people they meet. After weeks on the road, they arrive at the farm and struggle to find their place in the already established systems of work and friendships. John Rosen continues to execute his plan to bring down the United States, and President Massey comes out of hiding to regain control of his country, which is falling apart.

ALSO BY A. K. GENTRY

<u>Whitlow Series</u>
An Awkward Inheritance, Book 1
An Unlikely Partnership, Book 2
An Unforeseen Danger, Book 3

The Perfect Loophole

<u>Forewarned Series</u>
Unprepared, Book 1

ABOUT THE AUTHOR

A. K. Gentry grew up in rural North Carolina, USA. She has lived in small towns and rural areas all her life and loves bringing the small town values of faith and family to her writing.

Gentry is a retired registered nurse. She is married and has two daughters, one son-in-law, and two granddaughters.

www.ingramcontent.com/pod-product-compliance
Lightning Source LLC
Chambersburg PA
CBHW020756310726
48969CB00002B/569